# FIFER FOR THE UNION

# FIFER
# FOR THE
# UNION

## LORENZO ALLEN
## ILLUSTRATED BY
## BRIAN WILDSMITH

WILLIAM MORROW AND CO.
NEW YORK                1964

# For Helen Pillans and Helen Fay

Fourth Printing, February 1970

## TABLE OF CONTENTS

1    THE DAY THE BELLS RANG 9

2    MR. THRACE 22

3    TOO YOUNG 39

4    EMILY JANE 46

5    THE RUNAWAY 62

6    THE NEW RECRUIT 79

5

7 MR. PUTNAM 91

8 THE DRUM CORPS 98

9 GENERAL GOOBER 114

10 A SOLDIER'S DUTIES 130

11 "STRIKE TENTS!" 137

12 ON THE MARCH 143

13 THROUGH VIRGINIA 153

14 THE ADVANCE 168

15 TIRED, HUNGRY, AND COLD 183

16 BATTLE SMOKE 191

17 LOST 206

18 THE GOOBER GALOP 215

19 THE HOSPITAL 224

20 THE ORPHANAGE 237

21 EMILY JANE MEDDLES AGAIN 247

# FIFER
# FOR THE
# UNION

# 1     THE DAY THE BELLS RANG

Len Baldwin knew he'd always remember the bells. One of them started clanging from the tower of the Shrewsbury city hall. Then another joined it. Soon the school bell was going clickety-clack, and church bells with deep mellow notes were tolling solemnly, then whanging, as if their bell ropes were suddenly jerked by ringers too excited to toll. Every bell in town went to work within five or ten minutes, all at different speeds, rhythms, and pitches. It was enough to set people half-crazy.

Len stuck his head out of his bedroom window. The city must be on fire. He looked for smoke. The sky was clear toward the center of town. Out in the street the wagons, buggies, horseback riders, and pedestrians had stopped. The people looked as mystified as he felt. Then whistles from the factories and workshops began to scream—not to drown out the bells, it would seem, but because more noise was needed.

The frozen human statues sprang to life. The drivers whipped up their horses. The riders dug in spurs or slapped reins. Ladies and gentlemen on the sidewalks ran, clutching hats or skirts, shedding umbrellas and packages unheedingly, as they sprinted toward the city hall. People tore out of their houses and raced after them.

From the sounds inside his own house Len could tell that his mother and stepfather, Mr. Thrace, were dashing to the front door. A crash from the kitchen informed him that Edie, the hired girl, had dropped something, and was off for the street, too.

Len wasn't the last to move by any means. He reached the front sidewalk before anyone in the building. By climbing out his window, crossing the porch roof beneath it, and letting himself over the edge, where he hung for a minute with his fingers hooked, he dropped to the ground just as his stepfather ran down the front steps.

Mr. Thrace gave him an exasperated glance. He didn't say, "You'll break a leg!" but that was what he meant, Len was sure. He'd said it plenty of times before.

However, it was only a fleeting reflection on Len's part, as it must have been on Mr. Thrace's, he decided. The Old Bean looked very grave, rolled his head from side to side, and said to both Len and his wife, "It's come!"

Len understood immediately. For several months there'd been growing tension in the country. The people had been talking continuously about the rebellious Southern states. For a long time Len had been hearing that the South was getting ready for secession.

Why else had they been pinching off arsenals and forts for themselves? Len had read how they'd written themselves a provisional constitution for what they called "The Confederate States," and had even named a provisional president. Imagine the nerve of that! he'd thought. Everyone declared that the South had no right to do such a thing or even to consider secession.

President Lincoln had been inaugurated in March. Many times in Len's presence the speech had been quoted in which Lincoln had stated, "This government cannot endure permanently half slave and half free." He had said that the nation would end up, "All one thing, or all the other," but people believed it was little likely to become one thing or the other without the country's first going through war.

It was now April 12, in the year 1861. Len was sure the clangor meant only one thing: war.

"I'm going down there," he said, jerking his head in the direction of town.

"We'll all go," said Mr. Thrace, his voice melodious as always, but sounding tense now, as well.

At this moment Edie popped out of the house, wearing her apron. "I busted a crock!" she said to Mrs. Thrace, and ran past them.

To Len's surprise, his mother did not act as if she'd heard; yet she valued her blue-and-white crocks. She grasped her long calico skirts in one hand, to clear them of puddles, and ran also, disregarding her husband's proffered arm.

The street filled, as more and more people rushed from their houses. The bells continued wildly. Len's folks and Edie kept pace with him all the way to the city hall, where crowds had already gathered. Len saw members of the local band straggle up the steps in partial uniform, carrying their instruments and panting from the run they'd had from workshop or office.

What had happened?

He found out at once. Fort Sumter had been attacked.

The United States was in for trouble for sure, he told himself sagely.

When the bells stopped ringing, the silence overwhelmed Len. He felt as if he had suddenly become deaf. It was a relief the next second to see a breeze stir the tree leaves overhead, making them rustle. He heard them well, though the rustling was like a whisper.

Reassured about his hearing, he immediately transferred his anxiety to another thought. What was going to happen if the country went to war? How would people get along? Who'd take care of farms and factories if the men went away to fight? Women couldn't do men's work. They weren't strong enough.

Yet the men would have to go. The nation must be defended and kept whole. Everyone up here in the North saw that. Only those fool Southerners didn't, and were setting out to split the country by attacking Fort Sumter.

Len found himself growing so gloomy he almost felt ill.

Unnoticed by him, the band had got into place upon the platform. The men looked raggle-taggle in their mixture of uniforms and street or work clothes, but Len forgot the players' odd appearance when they burst out with a gay marching tune. His spirits lifted. They always did with music.

War had probably come, but his country would get through it all right. He felt comforted by the music and by the way people had turned out to get the news, showing they cared, and by the promptness with which the bells had rung, once the news had come.

He listened scornfully to the soapbox orators, who were shouting and haranguing in the crowd of people. The speakers were crepehangers, he thought. They said the North had better look out. It was in danger. The South was miles ahead of the Yankee states. The South had boundless amounts of arms and ammunition, due to raids it had been making on Southern forts. It had been buying war supplies abroad, too.

Len drifted to groups where the speeches were less dismal. He lost track of his mother and stepfather. Edie had totally disappeared in the crowd, her apron forgotten, her hands still floury.

Len wished his brother Will was still in Shrewsbury and could share all this excitement, but he'd been transferred from the drugstore in town, where he had been working, to a store in Philadelphia, run by his employer's son. He'd like to know how Will was reacting to today's news. Will didn't believe in slavery. He'd said so more than once.

How could his brother answer that bearded man on the soapbox? At this moment he was saying, "Us Yankees'll be a bunch of dumb fools if we fight to oppose slavery! I'm for it myself, by gum!"

A lot of people cheered, supporting him.

Another man was urging people to prepare to fight to get rid of slavery. Again listeners cheered.

Len didn't like finding out that both sides of the question had followers right here in his hometown.

He'd thought until now that people in Shrewsbury were like Will, and were opposed to slavery. If this was a general situation, the North would be divided in sentiment, just when it should be united, as the South was. If the attack on Fort Sumter brought on war between the states, then being divided would be a tremendous handicap to the North.

Len wandered around the rest of the day, even into the night. Finally hunger drove him home.

Two more days passed, during which the city, and indeed all of Massachusetts and the Northern states, waited in suspense for what was to come next.

What followed was the fall of Fort Sumter, far off in South Carolina.

Len heard everyone say, "Why didn't the garrison put up a fight?" Then the people learned that the men at the fort had lacked food and ammunition. They hadn't had a chance before their well-armed attackers.

Next came Lincoln's call for 75,000 men to defend the Union.

"I'll enlist!" Len shouted, his eyes shining.

His mother moaned.

Mr. Thrace immediately put his arm around her and said reassuringly, "He's too young. Just twelve. Don't be alarmed. Eighteen is the age limit." To Len he said disdainfully, "The president wants men, not boys. Can you see an army of boys going against those angry Southerners?"

Len tossed his head and glared sulkily at Mr. Thrace.

A day or so later he could hardly keep himself on the road to school. Everywhere he was confronted with the governor's posters, bearing the official call to arms. They fair made him itch to respond.

Out of nowhere, recruiting stations appeared. The local band, and others that drifted in from other towns, played all day long, and tramped up and down the main avenue in resplendent uniforms. People cheered the first recruits and called them heroes. They sang gaily in the streets when the band broke from military marches into "Old Dan Tucker," "Nellie Was a Lady," and "Oh, Susanna."

Now Len perceived a change in the mood of the townspeople. There was less discussion of slavery.

Instead, everyone angrily criticized the states that were turning or had turned disloyal to the Union. The secessionists were denounced as traitors.

"We'll fight them to the last man alive!" yelled a soapbox orator. His audience cheered.

Len heard people saying, "We must keep this nation one nation."

Len watched the recruits clop past him. They walked clumsily. He noted how differently the trained soldiers from the garrisons marched. They had a snap that thrilled him. He decided he'd walk like that hereafter, not go slouching along as before. He looked enviously at the smart uniforms, especially the bright blue of the Boston band, when it came through on parade with the famous leader, Gilmore, at its head.

He listened to the drums and bugles, the cornets and fifes, which the men played with such spirit that his heart soared. He felt a thrill when he saw the shining muskets laid over the shoulders of the soldiers following. With a proud expression he watched the cavalry prance down the street, each horse a splendor and each rider looking like a general.

He wrote to his brother Will, saying, "I hate the

South! I hope we wallop them till they scream!"

Will replied, "I don't hate the people of the South. It's not the right feeling to have for mistaken blunderers. They are plunging themselves into more sorrow than they know, poor fools. They must realize in their wayward souls that we are one nation, and should stay united just as a family should. Yet there they go, blasting us all apart, disregarding all that has gone before—the war for independence, the sacrifices and hardships of our forefathers. I feel disgust and dismay, even pity, but not hate.

"I've always wanted to be a doctor and save lives. I didn't tell you this before, because I saw I'd never have the money for study. Our father's early death ended that dream for me. I guess that is why I went to work for a druggist. It has been helpful. I have learned a lot about medicines and their uses."

Len stopped in surprise. A doctor? Will had wanted to become a doctor? Len had never guessed.

He read on. "President Lincoln seems to feel the war will not last long, since he's asked for enlistments for three months only. I hope he's right, but fear he may not be. However, I hope the war will be short so that there'll be less suffering among us. Also I hope it will pass over before you're old enough to get involved. I wouldn't like to see you as a soldier."

Oh, you wouldn't! Len thought indignantly. That's a fine wish! I suppose you think I wouldn't be any good. Or maybe you don't want anyone up North to tear into those Southerners and lambaste them, just because you don't hate them. Hmph! He looked at the letter with scorn, and added to himself, Even if they're nothing but fools, we've got to light into them, all of us, even *me*, and you should see that.

He continued reading. "I have given deep thought to my country's predicament, and wish to serve the nation where I will be most useful during the conflict, however long. For this reason, I have enlisted as a hospital steward."

Len stared in astonishment at the last line. What? Will had enlisted? Suddenly he felt immensely proud of his brother. Will had lost no time answering the call. He was among the first to volunteer. That showed a marvelous patriotic spirit. All of his life Will would be able to hold his head high, because he'd responded at once when his country needed him. Len glowed with admiration for his brother.

Then he clenched his fists in despair. He wanted

to enlist too—he had wanted to the day Lincoln had called for recruits. Probably that was the day Will had volunteered. The very same day! But who had squashed Len with a big *no*? Mr. Old Bean Thrace, saying he was too young, saying the president wanted men, not boys. Oh, if only he were twenty-one, like Will, or eighteen, which was the age accepted without question by the army. Why was he only twelve? Why was it his fate to be forced to stay home and live it out with a stepfather and do nothing, absolutely nothing, for his beloved country?

Never had he felt more dismal, or loved the United States so much.

# 2                  MR. THRACE

Len had been eight years old when his father died. His whole life changed overnight. His father had been his idol, whom he'd followed around so much, especially when just a little fellow, that his father had nicknamed him Shadow.

His father had taught him to whittle. Len still possessed the good knife he had given him. He had played games with him and Will. He'd read to the family in the evening, with Len always on a stool beside him, Will at the table idly drawing, and their mother crocheting under the soft yellow light of the lamp. He remembered his father's teasing, his jokes, his kind understanding.

Then suddenly there had been a blank around Len and a cold place inside him. He felt lost and alone. He crept to his mother, but it was not the same. She, too, felt lost and alone. She dressed herself in black mourning, as was the custom, but he could not understand the change it made in her appearance. She had always looked beautiful in her colored gowns and bonnets, which set off the delicate tints of her skin and her blond hair, and brought out the blue of her eyes. Now the dull black made her ghostly looking. She was suffering, too, from the shock of her husband's death, but Len didn't understand why she sometimes turned from him and shut herself up alone in her room to cry. He did not know that she was trying to spare him. He just felt he was losing, or had lost, her also.

Will had been a little comfort, but Will was nine years older. He took a job almost at once, and was away from the house except at night. He was always preoccupied with his own affairs.

For days Len had wandered about the house and

garden, feeling queer and out of sorts. Gradually he became adjusted to the change, although not entirely, for even now he occasionally had touches of unhappiness, which he could not explain, but which stemmed from the upset caused by his father's death.

Time passed. His mother became more cheerful. They were good friends; he had fun with her. But she was busy, for she'd had to start earning their living. He remembered the sewing, the yards and yards of cloth and lace strewn over the chairs and worktable, and his mother's head, bent over the tiny stitches she was taking. She was sewing herself half-blind, her eyes smarting as she tried to finish pieces of work in the fading light of a winter day.

And the black clothes! Always the black, dismal clothes.

Then gradually bits of white appeared at her wrists and neck, then bands of blue or rose, then one day a beautiful new dress of pale green. How lovely she looked! He could remember that, because it had made him feel much better to have her looking like her old self again. Perhaps he was ten by then.

Then, in a little while, Mr. Thrace began to call. Len didn't pay much attention to his visits, although he sometimes went along when Mr. Thrace took his mother out for a drive. He did not think of him. The man was kind to him, sometimes gave him a little pocket money or books of maxims or leaflets of nature lore.

Len was quite astonished when his mother said one day, "Len dear, I want to prepare you to receive a new father."

"I don't want a new father," he had said.

"But, dear, you'd be so much better off, and he's such a good, kind man. He will do all in his power to help you grow into a fine person."

"Who will?" he cried.

"Mr. Thrace."

"What do you mean?"

"He has asked me to marry him. I find that I love him. I have consented."

Len felt surprise more than anything else. It wasn't until after his mother and he and Will had moved to Mr. Thrace's large house that he began to feel uneasy. Mr. Thrace had said, "Call me Father."

Will had complied at once.

Len had said, "You're not my father! I've got a father of my own."

Mr. Thrace had said, "I'll not insist on that now, but I want you to look on me as a father. I regard you and Will as my sons, and will do my duty by you. Will needs my help less, because he is a young man now. It is you I will try to guide to a full, good life, for your mother's sake."

Len didn't feel he needed to be guided to a full, good life. Wasn't he doing all right, just eating, sleeping, doing a few daily chores, going to school? Just growing by himself? It sounded bad, this suggestion that he might be interfered with. He didn't like the way his mother smiled and nodded in approval. It was as if she was turning him over to this man, instead of keeping her hand on him herself.

Len had flared up at the first task Mr. Thrace assigned him. "Will you sweep off the veranda, please?"

"Mama didn't tell me to," Len said.

"Len dear," his mother advised, "you must mind Mr. Thrace. He is your stepfather and legal guardian now, you know."

That was two years back. Since then it had been hammer and tongs between stepfather and boy most of the time. Mr. Thrace believed in discipline. He believed boys should have chores and responsibilities, that they should use good grammar and clean language and be respectful to their elders. He had made it very clear that Len must obey him and be polite to him at all times.

Len had made it clear that he had other ideas, but he'd had to give in. He didn't want to battle all the time. It made his mother too unhappy. Besides, rebelling just led to punishment. Gradually he learned to get along with fewer clashes, but he kept himself aloof and unfriendly toward Mr. Thrace. Doing this helped him hide the fact that he continued to smolder inside. Nowadays the cold relationship did not bother him much, unless Mr. Thrace objected to something Len craved, such as enlisting in the army.

Len put Will's letter into his desk and crawled out his window to drop off the veranda roof. He couldn't stand being inside the house any longer. He had to do something or he'd burst.

Out in the street he found a stick and began whacking leaves off the hedges with it as he went along. He kicked at stones and walked with head down, saying over and over to himself, "I want to enlist, too!"

He barely noticed where he walked, so was considerably startled when he ran smack into a horse. The animal was grazing on curbside grass, his body across the sidewalk. The rope with which he had been tethered hung loose from his neck, the end strands looking as if he'd jerked himself free.

Len was acquainted with most of the horses in his neighborhood. They were more or less his personal friends. He went frequently to stables along the street to pet the animals and to feed them carrots. He often helped a neighbor with his harnessing. Sometimes, to oblige a friend, he would drive a man's rig downtown to bring him home from work.

This horse was a stranger, a rich chestnut in color, his mane clipped and standing erect, his eyes mellow and friendly in expression. He was probably used to boys. Len picked up the trailing rope and glanced about. Few people were on the street at this moment. No one seemed to be looking for a horse. Len wasn't sure what to do with it.

He could ride it around bareback. This was a sport he rarely got, for Mr. Thrace did not own a horse. Len mounted. Pressing on the horse's neck with his hands and pushing with one knee or the other against the animal's sides, he directed him down the street at a jolly pace. On the way no one called out, claiming the horse. He caused quite a stir in the buggy traffic as he pounded past. One carriage horse shied, and he heard a faint scream from the lady driver inside.

He didn't want to ride through the center of town. Without reins, he knew that he didn't have sure control of the animal. People crossed the streets where they pleased. Children and dogs were apt to run into his path. He urged the horse off the main street to a placid square of green grass, edged with giant elms. At one side rose the slender steeple and white walls of a church. He pulled his mount to a stop with jerks on the frayed rope and slid off his back.

For a moment he stroked the long nose. If only he had a horse like this. Whose was it, anyway? The owner couldn't be a very careful type, tying him up the way he had. He couldn't care much, or he wouldn't let a horse like this out of his sight. Smart animal, too. Obeyed orders, caught on fast to what a rider wanted. Bet there was a lot Len could make him do, like—like—Len looked around for possibilities.

There were eight or nine steps leading up to the church door. "Ever been to church, boy?" he asked the horse, and thought, I wish the Old Bean could see what I'm going to do.

He led the horse across the grass and started to make him go up into the church. "We'll give the Old Bean a shock," he informed the animal. "The whole town, too. I can just see it. Come on, boy, go on up the steps."

But he gave up. He discovered two ladies in fine silk dresses and velvet bonnets coming. They stared to see a horse standing on the walk in their way. They stared hard at Len, too, showing disapproval.

He tugged at the rope, pulled his steed back into the street, and let the women pass. Then he remembered that there was a flight of steps leading into the church basement. The basement would have to do. It wouldn't be quite so funny to take the horse there, but he could prolong the prank. He'd leave him there for the night, and then let him loose in the morning, when the factory people were walking past to work. He himself would crawl out of the basement through a back window and go watch the crowd discover the horse. That'd be a laugh. If he couldn't join the army, he'd do something to shake up the town. He had to do *something*, or he'd go crazy, he felt so awful.

He pushed the reluctant horse through the basement door, then pulled him to the staircase and urged him down. The animal didn't seem to have any system for stairs at all. His feet went everywhere. He cracked several steps in sheer clumsiness and made a ghastly clatter besides. He didn't like going down steps, that was clear. He backed and skittered and whinnied with fear. It was all Len could do to get him to the bottom.

Len was panting when they finally reached the room below the church. It was divided, by movable partitions, into little cells. Each cell was filled with neat rows of chairs for the Sunday-school groups that met there every Sunday before church services.

The horse was still frightened, and twitched nervously. Len spent several moments soothing him. He turned him around in the narrow passage left by the partitions. The horse knocked over several chairs.

Len led him to a pillar and tied him to it. As soon as he felt that the horse was calm again and apparently no longer afraid of his strange surroundings, he decided he could safely leave. It was getting late, and he was starving for supper and for the raisin pie he'd seen Edie baking. A big chunk of pie would hit the right spot today. He needed something extra good if he was ever going to feel better.

Len gave the horse a fond pat and ran back up the stairs.

He slept heavily that night, so heavily, in fact, that he overslept, and woke up with a feeling of bewilderment. What was it he had to hustle out and tend to before—before—? It was something about factory workers.

Jehoshaphat! The horse!

He must let him out of the church basement as the workers came past, or miss all the fun. That meant *now*, right now! Later, there'd be only a few people on the street. Now was the best time. He might even be late, but he thought not. Not if he hurried.

He sprang out of bed, tossed his nightclothes on the floor, and jumped into his shirt and trousers. Clutching his shoes in his hand, he tiptoed out into the hall to go silently down the stairs. He heard a door close below. There was a smell of breakfast in the air. He'd be late for breakfast.

He shrugged. So he'd be late. The Old Bean would make remarks. He was very insistent on prompt attendance at meals.

Len listened a minute for the clink of dishes. There wasn't a sound. He probably had plenty of time. Going a little faster, he slipped down the carpeted staircase, reached the lower hall, and was just ready to sprint outside, when the dining-room door opened and Mr. Thrace glowered at him, his brown eyes looking unusually fierce.

"Young man, come in here," he said.

The table was set for breakfast, but the food had not yet been brought in. A ledger lay at Mr. Thrace's place, along with papers, pen and ink, and a few pieces of currency. Len shuffled into the room, chafing at the delay.

"Put on your shoes." Mr. Thrace's rich voice was scornful. "Only a coward sneaks out of his home." He looked inquiringly at Len, as he added, "Or perhaps you have a praiseworthy reason, such as not wanting to disturb sleeping members of the family."

"Yes." Len snatched at this explanation. He quickly put on his shoes, then sank into his chair at the table and rumpled his hair.

"Actually," his stepfather said dryly, "everyone is awake before you today. Now sit up properly, boy! You and I are going to have a serious talk. Breakfast has been put off till we settle certain affairs between us. Now then—" He picked up a pen and toyed with it. "I've had three recent talks with your schoolmaster. I told you last month you would have to mend your ways. I warned you. Mr. Ash again reports absences, a regrettable amount of unruliness in the schoolroom, and a poor study record. You're not trying. I told you to try, did I not?"

"Yup."

"I'd prefer you to use the word, yes, plus sir. It is more courteous to your elders to add a sir, you know. Why are you cutting school?"

"Why are you snooping on what I do?" Len asked. "I can run my own life."

Mr. Thrace looked stonily over Len's head, as if he hadn't spoken. "Don't you realize a boy must fit himself in every way possible for his life as a man? Many a boy in this country would give his hand to have your chance at schooling. Consider our president and his early struggles even to possess a book."

"I've heard all that."

"What is the matter with you then?"

"Nothing."

"Then why—?"

"There is no why!" Len swung the hair out of his eyes with an angry toss of the head.

Mr. Thrace slapped the pen down onto the table. "This is to stop, young man. By that I mean neglecting studies, playing hooky, stirring up mischief in the classroom, and interrupting classwork. By that I also mean being as impudent as you dare to me! When I became your mother's husband, I became your legal guardian, and I am responsible for your correct upbringing. I shall spare no effort to bring you to heel, I assure you. Do you understand now?"

"Yup."

"What did I say to say?"

"Yes-plus-sir, sir," Len said rapidly, screwing his mouth over the words with as much mockery as he could get into them.

"You young cub. Say 'Yes, sir,' simply and clearly, as you know I intended."

"Yes, sir." He spoke in a falsetto voice this time, and grinned to himself at the flicker of anger in Mr. Thrace's eyes.

When his stepfather spoke again, his rich voice had an edge. "Sit up straight. You behave like a slouch. You are trying to anger me. Well, it won't work. I know my duty, and I'll teach you yours. You'll thank me one day, Son."

"I'm not your son!"

"Then who is to be responsible for this twelve-year-old rebel? You cannot turn to your mother for guidance, for you do not heed her either."

"I do so."

"Not one bit of it. It is she who longs to have you in school, and who wants you growing up fine and manly and obedient. Reflect, boy! How do you behave in general? I've never encountered more disregard for your elders than you've been showing everywhere lately. Even Will remarked about your quarrelsome ways the last time he was home."

"Leave Will out of this! You snoop into my affairs, because you think you've *got* me. Well, you haven't got *Will!* He's twenty-one, and can run his own life forever. He can *enlist!*" With that, Len leaped for the door.

With as swift a bound, Mr. Thrace reached Len's side, grasped him with a grip of iron, and said, "I've not excused you yet. There is one other matter. The horse you took down into the church basement."

At the unexpected mention of the horse, Len grew rigid. Someone had made a discovery, and had come tattling. He decided to be very cautious. Avoiding his stepfather's eyes, he repeated innocently, "Horse?"

"Yes, horse."

Len took up the study of fly specks on the ceiling.

"The room is a shambles. All the screens broken, the chairs smashed. He must have kicked and raged around all night."

Len's gaze dodged to the lace curtain over the window.

"Look at me directly, young man!"

Reluctantly Len turned his glance to his step-father's, and found it blazing at him in a white fire of indignation and exasperation.

Mr. Thrace raised his hand and cuffed Len severely. "You know what that is for?" he asked.

"For putting the horse in the basement."

"No. It is to cure you of some of your impudence, and if I don't see results, Len Baldwin, I shall take drastic measures. I mean what I say. Now go upstairs and wash your hands, comb your hair, and return immediately. We shall start breakfast. Then off you go to school—and you are going to study, young man, mark my words!"

How did the Old Bean find out? Len wondered, as he stumbled upstairs. He heard his mother come from the kitchen and enter the dining room. His stepfather's resonant voice, although kept low-pitched, drifted up with the answer. "Two women, passing the church, saw him with the animal. I shall pay the damages, of course."

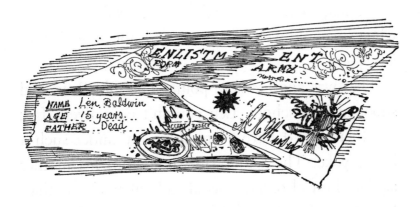

ENLISTMENT FORM
ARMY

NAME Len Baldwin
AGE 15 years
FATHER Dead

**3**                                          **TOO YOUNG**

Len was in a frenzy all day. I hate him, he kept telling himself. He's getting worse and worse, bearing down on me, telling me what I must do, prying into my affairs.

It did not help him to reflect that his behavior that morning had not done much to put him in the right. The Old Bean had accused him of impudence and of trying to goad him to anger, and that was correct. Len tossed his head and set his jaw stubbornly, excusing himself. Any fellow would act like that, burdened with a tyrant stepfather. Why couldn't Mr. Thrace let him alone?

He brooded over his wrongs during history, geography, and arithmetic—in fact, every lesson. He mumbled, "I don't know," to Mr. Ash's questions, when he could well have answered, for he had studied.

That was another sore point. The Old Bean had snooped into school. Len couldn't even live a free life there. He'd have years of misery under such a heavy yoke. The Old Bean would turn his mother against him also. He was already at work on that, Len told himself. He'd have to ask permission to breathe finally, he predicted gloomily.

Len clenched his fists. He'd fight him. He'd not take it. He'd show Mr. Thrace who was running Len's affairs for him. It would be Len, not a stepfather! Boys and stepfathers were natural-born enemies.

It was nearly time for school to let out. He'd have to go back to his jail sentence and the mean jailer. Suddenly a wild, exciting thought took fire inside him. By Jove! Why had it never occurred to him before? It held the answer to all his problems. It was exactly what he wanted to do, besides. It meant escape from tyranny, blissful freedom from constant discipline and criticism.

He felt so cheered that he jumped into the spelling match that ended the classwork each day, and spelled down everyone in the room.

"Well!" Mr. Ash exclaimed. "Did you suddenly wake up?"

"Yes, *sir!*" Len cried.

He leaped out the door the minute class was dismissed. He walked rapidly down the street, heading into the center of town, where flags were flying and the large brown tents of the recruiting stations stood. He'd hung around them more than once, watching men enlist. He'd run errands for the officers. A lieutenant had said invitingly, "You wouldn't want to join up, would you?" But he had winked at a fellow officer, so Len had known he was joking and had not replied.

The governor's posters still urgently exhibited their call to arms in bold letters. *Here* was where he belonged. His country needed him. At home no one cared. He'd enlist just like Will. Mr. Thrace would have to give in and let him go. Len would find a way to make him.

He felt increasingly nervous as he neared the station. Some of the men hanging about were twice his size. Some had beards, and looked three or four times older. They were big and strong. They were *men*. And he was a boy, not even the age yet at which the army began accepting boy recruits. Yet one of his schoolmates had made it recently. The boy was fifteen, but not much taller or older-looking than Len. He'd made it.

Len drew himself up straight, slowed his pace, tried to look very businesslike, rather than eager. They needed soldiers. Well, here was their chance to get one. He went into the tent. An officer in charge gave him a paper to fill out. He barely glanced at Len. So far so good.

The paper presented problems. He wrote down his name, address, height, and weight, and carefully printed fifteen as his age. Then he saw he must give the name and address of his next of kin. That meant parents, which was awkward. "Father dead," he wrote, and hoped no questions would be asked about

his mother. Other spaces were to be filled in by ex-
amining officers. He scanned them anxiously, hoping
he'd not be betrayed by anything listed there.

"I'm ready, sir," he said, handing his paper to an
orderly.

The orderly glanced over it, and said, "Right this
way. I'll conduct you to the general."

The general. Phew! Len drew a long breath. It
looked as if he'd made it on the first step, else they
would not take him to the general. He felt himself
grow shaky inside. He could hardly keep his legs from
wobbling or his lips from quivering. Clenching his
fists and trying to keep his back poker-stiff, he
clopped after the orderly into another tent.

A bearded man, with eyes gleaming from under
bristly eyebrows, sat waiting at the farther end. Officers stood near his table. A band of recruits were at
one side behind a rope. They were men—not boys.
Some had bushy beards like the general's, and they
were big fellows, brawny, almost giants in contrast
with Len.

With his jaw set so tight his teeth hurt, Len walked
forward. The general glanced at him, then looked up
at the orderly, who was presenting Len's paper.

"What's *this?*" the general demanded.

"A recruit, sir!" the orderly answered, and saluted briskly.

The general sprang to his feet, raised both fists, and waved them with frenzy. "Take the little shrimp out of this tent! We've no need for infants in this brigade!" he roared.

Loud guffaws burst from the line of recruits.

"Silence!" the orderly shouted, but no one listened to him. The whole tent seemed to flap up and down with raucous laughs.

Len snatched his paper off the table and fled, his face flaming, his ears burning. Why had he done it? He might have known.

He raced out of the recruiting area. He fancied he could hear the laughter spreading, as the news went from man to man and from tent to tent. He dashed around the nearest building, then sped along an alley until he was far from the tents and the witnesses of the embarrassing episode. He still held the paper, the sad reminder of his humiliation. He glared at it in distaste, then tore it into shreds and buried the pieces in mud at the side of the road.

He was glad he'd gone alone to enlist. Perhaps the

news would not spread beyond the recruiting station. He could not bear for the boys at school to learn what the general had said.

He knew he was crushed by more than the humiliation. His problem at home was not solved. He had lost the only possible means of escape from his cruel, heartless stepfather.

# 4                                       EMILY JANE

As Len drifted homeward with hanging head, he paid no attention to the road, just stumbled along on the board sidewalk or wandered into the street itself, where he kicked irritably at chunks of mud, sending them flying into the mirrorlike puddles left by a recent rain. He only half heard the swift clopping of a horse's hooves, until he realized that the animal was coming with greater speed than seemed natural. He looked around.

He saw a horse and buggy tearing toward him at

a frightful pace, despite the deep oozy mud. From
time to time the conveyance went through a puddle.
Len saw a shower of water arch out, flooding the side
of the road. He was about to shelter himself behind
a tree when he noticed the person in the buggy, a
young woman, jouncing about so uncontrollably she
was likely to be pitched out. Whenever the wheels
dropped into a rut, her feet appeared over the dashboard. One arm clutched her bonnet. With her other
hand she held something against her. A baby? he
wondered. Then he saw it was a dog.

The horse galloped madly, his eyes wild and staring. Clearly he was running away, and in no time
would endanger the occupants of the buggy. Let the
wheel once hit a rock, and the whole thing would
break up or tip over. The horse must be stopped. Len
set himself, half crouched, beside the road and
waited. "Whoa!" he yelled.

He lunged for the horse's neck, seized the straps
and reins, pushed his foot into the right-hand shaft,
heaved himself up, and was carried through mud and
puddles. Fountains of brown water poured over him.

The horse's breathing was harsh and desperate. It
was plain he was reaching a fatigue point. Soon he

began to slow down. Len's grip on the bridle also had effect. In a short time the horse stopped in a welter of mud almost knee-deep.

Len clung to him. He freed his foot from the shaft, and noted a torn trouser leg and blood flowing from a cut. He stood in the mud, swaying dizzily a moment, then began soothing the animal, stroking him and talking quietly. He heard squeakings and faint screams from the person in the buggy and then the yapping of the little dog.

"Oh dear! I think I shall swoon!" the young woman cried. She leaned back in the seat with her hand pressed to her forehead. The little dog, a terrier, stood on her lap and barked nervously.

"You're all right, ma'am," Len said. "Just let me get your horse calmed down, and I'll help you."

The young lady opened her eyes, and he saw that they were wide and blue. She was perhaps somewhere near Will's age. She was pretty, even though her hair tumbled every which way and her face was spotted with mud. Her elegant dress was also spotted.

"Oh! Oh! Oh!" the young lady exclaimed, but in a stronger voice. A little color crept into her face.

Len worked with the horse a while longer, glancing

occasionally at the young woman in the buggy. He noticed that she was now smoothing down her skirts and looking in horror at the muddy spots on her dress.

She pushed the little dog off her lap. "Bad dog!" she said. "You frightened Duke with your barking and snapping. Bad, bad dog!" She fastened her large eyes on Len. "Sir, I do believe you saved our lives. . . . Why, you're only a boy! I thought it was a man who dashed up like that. How ever did you stop that mad horse? Wait till I tell my cousin Steven the kind of horse he lent me to drive home from Grandmama's. I'll never forgive him!"

"He's high-strung," said Len. "You have to watch out when you drive this kind of horse. Keep a tight rein on him."

"I just couldn't pull the mean old thing up! He knew only too well he was on his way home. So what did he do? When I attempted to slow him, he decided to shy at fence posts and bushes, even a goat. He tried me beyond all patience. I tied the reins to the dashboard, but they got loose. I whipped him. Then Snip began to bark—you bad dog, yes, you did —and Duke took off. It's a wonder I didn't faint, don't you think?"

"The way the buggy was jumping around, it's a wonder you weren't dumped out into the road and hurt."

The young lady screamed. "Dumped out? Oh, my hamper! Where is it? And my best dress inside it. Oh dear, dear, dear! The hamper was right here, right beside me on the seat when we started."

"I think Duke has settled down now." Len waded toward her, holding the reins. He checked the buckles and straps of the harness as he approached the buggy. Everything had held. The young lady was lucky, luckier than she realized, he thought.

He held the reins out to her.

"I shan't touch them!" she cried.

"But you have to."

"I'm too shaken. I couldn't possibly drive that animal again. Sir, please help me."

What was he to do? She was sure she couldn't control the horse herself. She certainly needed someone.

"Move over," he said, and climbed into the rig, his torn pant leg flapping, his cut flowing dark red over the mud splashed on his bare leg.

He turned the horse and went back down the road

to hunt for the hamper. They found it lying beside a drainage ditch some distance away. It was not badly damaged, and its leather straps were still tightly fastened. With cries of delight the girl received it and proceeded to open it.

"Oh, goody! Grandmama wrapped everything in lots of paper. Everything's all right. And here's a lovely surprise! Food! Let's eat something this minute. I was never more hungry." She broke into a package, and produced a sandwich of buttered homemade bread and a thick slab of beef, which she handed him. "Do have a pickle," she cried, thrusting one into his mouth. "And there's cake, too, if you like. And pie!"

"Pfft!" he exclaimed, hands clutching bread and the reins, and his mouth stopped shut with a pickle.

She tittered. "Oh, you do look funny! All that mud on your face. And a green cigar. What's your name, boy?"

He managed to pull out the pickle for a reply. "Len Baldwin. What's yours?"

"I'm Emily Jane Bradford. I'm eighteen years old. You wouldn't have heard of my father, would you? Judge Leonias Bradford?"

"No."

She sighed. "No, I suppose not. Yet he is really quite famous. Sure you didn't hear about him? He has written a whole book by himself about slavery and what a wrong it is."

"I didn't hear about it," he said, "but then, I don't read books much."

She pouted as if in reproach, and he began to wish he read more, or at least had read her father's book. But then she shrugged prettily, and said, "I haven't read it either. Isn't that wicked? My very own father. Down, boy, down!" She pushed the little dog. He had smelled the meat, and was standing on his hind legs, his front paws on Len's knees. He barked for food. "You can't have one bite. You are a bad dog!"

They finished their sandwiches. Len slipped the dog a bite or two to pacify him, then gently flipped the reins to start the horse along the way.

"Will you drive me clear home, Len?" Emily Jane asked, her blue eyes ever so wistful.

"I guess so. How far is it?"

"You'll see. You go straight along this turnpike. Duke knows when to turn off. Oh, I'm so glad you will do it. You can't imagine how it relieves me. And look at the mud on my dress! I suppose I must let it dry, then rub it off."

She began fussing with her hair, then her bonnet, straightening its flowers and ribbons. Then, as the mud spots on her dress dried, she dusted and brushed her skirts as busily as a little housewife in her parlor. She did not talk much, but hummed snatches of songs.

Len felt himself enjoying the drive more and more, despite the prickings of conscience that reminded him that Mr. Thrace and his mother would think, when he returned very late—and he undoubtedly would—that he was doing it on purpose as a result of the fuss this morning.

He lifted his chin cockily. That was what they'd think, and he'd let them. He wouldn't explain. Well, maybe he would privately to his mother. He had no quarrel with her. He didn't wish to make her anxious. He'd explain and apologize.

Having made this decision, he drove along contentedly, hardly noticing his companion until she began to stir about. She looked hastily over her shoulder. He became aware of the *plokity-plok* of hoofbeats and the rattling sound made by an approaching vehicle, which was about to overtake them.

"Oh dear! I wonder how I look." Emily Jane pushed Snip off her lap, patted her skirts, fluffed the ruffles on her waist, and fussed with her bonnet. "The stagecoach is about to pass us," she announced. "I might know somebody on board."

Len glanced back at the swift-moving coach. It was drawn by six handsome black horses. The driver was splendid in a green coat, opened to reveal a scarlet vest, and brass buttons. Len pulled to the side to make room. The passengers peered from the windows. All young men. When they beheld Emily Jane, they waved their top hats in large sweeping gestures to salute her, and cried, "Happy journey, Miss!" Then they cheered.

The driver cracked his whip. His eyes flashed at her, and he smiled flirtatiously. "Yahoo!" he bellowed, cracked the whip again, and drove onward at a mad pace.

Emily Jane sighed with great contentment. "Aren't they silly young gentlemen?"

She settled herself again, took Snip onto her lap, and leaned back against the seat. For a long while she did not move, not even to stroke the dog. Len found this enjoyable, too. All her scratching and fussing had reminded him of a little hen.

Suddenly she slumped down against him, her head coming to rest on his shoulder.

"Hey!" he said. "Get away!" Oh, for heaven's sake! The girl was asleep, and was so much bigger than he that he felt as if a mountain were leaning against him. "Wake up!" he said, but halfheartedly. He'd better endure it for a while. She was probably extremely tired. She was a nice person, but awfully silly in some ways. He wondered what Will would think of a girl like Emily Jane.

Duke trotted along sedately, with the air of a horse who had never in his life kicked up his heels and run away. They went on and on. Len didn't know how many minutes or hours spun by. The clouds had turned gray, darkening the sky. The sun was hidden. He felt hungry again, so several hours must have passed.

"Wake up!" he said once, and shifted his aching shoulder so that Emily Jane's head bobbed up and down in a most uncomfortable manner. She wouldn't sleep much longer that way, he guessed. But she did, and he drove onward, saying nothing, growing sleepy himself.

When he awoke it was dark. Duke had dragged the buggy into a meadow. Len didn't know how long they'd been there. They seemed to be near a city, for he saw lighted windowpanes from clusters of houses.

"Wake up!" He poked Emily Jane urgently.

Her eyelids fluttered, then her body stretched out as straight as possible in the cramped space. "Ouch!" she said loudly, and rubbed her neck. "It's broken! Ouch!"

"Where do you live?" he demanded. "I hope we haven't passed it."

"Oh no," she answered, looking about and smiling reassuringly. "Just one or two more miles. Give Duke his head. He'll take us there."

Len was uneasy. The journey had taken longer than he'd expected. He still had a long trip back. It occurred to him he had no ride home.

"How do I get home?" he asked.

"Don't you worry. My father, Judge Leonias Bradford, will tend to that."

"I won't get home till after midnight. My folks'll explode."

"You'll get back in good time. Sometime tomorrow on the stage."

"I have to get back tonight."

"Nonsense! You can't go tonight. There's no conveyance. Now stop worrying, I said. My father, Judge Leonias Bradford, will tell your father all the trouble you went to. It will all be explained, and no one will mind at all."

"You don't know my— He isn't my father. He's a stepfather."

"Doesn't matter. Father, stepfather, grandfather, any kind of father—the minute he reads the note that I'll ask my father to write, he will forgive all."

When they reached the large stone house in which Emily Jane lived, Mrs. Stebbins, the housekeeper, fluttered out excitedly, and said, "Oh, Miss Emily Jane! Your father has been summoned to Washington. He packed, and was off on the stage in fifteen minutes this morning."

"Oooh!" Emily Jane drew out the sound in a long ecstatic sigh. "To Washington! How utterly wonderful! He's been sent for to confer with the president, I would guess. Oh! How proud that makes me!" She turned to Len. "It's all on account of the letter he wrote, offering his services in the recruitment department. Father has been much disturbed that the quotas aren't reached more swiftly. The North needs thousands of enlistments, he says over and over."

Len did not listen. All he could think of was that he wanted to return home with as little delay as possible, and now her father was gone. He did not want to face his stepfather without the letter of explanation from Emily Jane's father. He'd been counting on it. It was true he'd had the bold idea of keeping silent, refusing to explain, except perhaps to his mother. But common sense warned him that this would just get him into trouble unnecessarily.

He realized now that since the army had turned him down, he'd have to live with the Old Bean until he was grown, and it would be smarter to be right rather than wrong, good rather than bad. That way his stepfather wouldn't have a chance again to get the best of him. Any arguments or scraps they'd have from now on would just show how unreasonable, demanding, and autocratic the man was. So he must not only hurry back, he must have a note of explanation. Emily Jane would have to write it.

He heard her say to Mrs. Stebbins, "Light a lamp, please, and show this small brave man up to the east bedroom."

Small brave man, he echoed to himself. It sounded wonderful to be called "brave." Better yet, "man." But he wished she hadn't used the word, "small."

"He saved my life," she went on, "with complete disregard for his own. At great risk he stopped Duke, who was running away. He's a hero!"

Len was pleased to see how deeply impressed Mrs. Stebbins appeared to be by this news.

"Len," Emily Jane added, "the stage leaves at five thirty tomorrow. Mrs. Stebbins will call you in time and give you breakfast. Here is your fare." She handed him some coins, drawn from her reticule. "I can't tell you how deeply grateful I am. I want to reward you. What can I do?"

Len shrugged. "Nothing."

"Nonsense! My father, Judge Leonias Bradford, will think I am most remiss. He will never forgive me if I let you go without a reward of some kind. What a shame he's involved with recruitment just now."

Recruitment? Len now caught the word. "I know what I want! I want to enlist. I applied at home, but the army turned me down."

Her eyes grew round. "They did? They must be mad! That's proof of what my father said, that they are turning away too many volunteers because of fussy regulations. My father says the North needs every last soldier it can get." A smile of inspiration broke over her face. "I know what to do! I'll get my father to help you. As a head recruitment officer, he should have much influence, and be able to place you in the army. He'll be pleased to, when he hears how brave you are. The army needs brave men. Now give me the information about yourself that I must have."

Len had so recently filled out an enlistment document that he knew what statistics he must supply. They were practically burned into his soul. He emphasized that his father was dead and that his stepfather cared not at all what he did, and would probably be glad to have him off his hands. Fearful of the army regulations concerning age, he took no chances. He told her he was fifteen.

She took notes, then yawned daintily. "Oh dear, how sleepy I am! I must say good-night. You'll be up and gone tomorrow before I open my eyes, but I'll write my father directly I've finished breakfast. It's a promise. I know my father, Judge Leonias Bradford, will not fail us."

She then dashed off a note to Len's stepfather to explain his absence and to express her gratitude. As he pushed it into his pocket, his fingers touched on a small rooster he'd been carving. He drew it out. "You can have this, if you want."

Her little screeches of joy were worth a dozen thank-you's. He swelled with pride when she said, "I didn't know you were a talented as well as a brave young gentleman."

## 5                THE RUNAWAY

The school term ended. The war news grew more and more absorbing, but also more disturbing. Len was filled with anxiety. Things weren't going well with the Northern troops.

Newspapers published accounts of every skirmish between the Northern and Confederate armies. The president had ordered a blockade of Southern ports, hoping to keep the Rebels from obtaining supplies. The newssheets reported failures of the Northern navy. These failures were little understood, until realization came that the North barely had a navy and must build ships at once. In fact, to carry out the president's command, ferryboats had been taken to sea, but had sunk under Rebel shelling.

General Winfield Scott had been training 50,000 recruits near Washington. These men were probably the rawest ever to enter an army. Many had never handled a gun. They did not know how to march, hold formation, or obey orders. They were not used to roughing it in encampments with scanty equipment and comfort. They thought that their three-month enlistment meant a few brief encounters with the Rebels, followed by a quick victory. Why bother with all the routine and the discipline and the orders to march and drill all day long? Although they were patriotic and wished to protect the Union, they weren't soldiers at heart.

By July, despite the general's efforts, the troops were not properly prepared for the Confederate attack that occurred on the twenty-first at Bull Run in Virginia. People in the Northern states were not prepared to learn that General Scott's army had been hopelessly licked, in fact, had turned and fled, rushing into Washington with the enemy in hot pursuit.

With such a defeat as this, the Union was in danger of being wiped out, people now realized. The whole North rocked with the disaster.

McClellan was put in charge of the army in Virginia. The three-month recruits of the first period of enlistment went home or reenlisted, but now all soldiers were signed in for three years.

Bull Run had badly shaken the Northern states. People now saw that every effort must be made to win. Men must be rigorously trained, too. There must be no more playing at war, with ladies and gentlemen, dressed to the nines in their best clothes, driving out to a shore of the Potomac in the afternoon to watch skirmishes across the river. The North must manufacture guns, cannon, and ships, extend the railroads, build wagon roads, provide the rations for a great army, and, most of all, raise one so vast that it could overwhelm the South in sheer size alone.

Len read the papers and watched hundreds of newly enlisted men march past on their way to training camps. He felt horrible.

The days moved along, one by one, each bringing disappointment, because no big document arrived in the mail with his name on it. Then one day, when he looked into the box, he did find a large envelope. He seized it and raced upstairs to his room.

It was from the War Department. It contained his acceptance papers into the Army of the United States for three years as a musician.

A musician! He was startled. Then he remembered that the army took younger enlistees for the military bands.

He was ordered to present himself to the Headquarters of Company D, in Boston, on August 1, for immediate departure south. His age was listed as fifteen. The papers were signed by Judge Leonias Bradford.

Len dropped into a chair, feeling as if his legs had become too flabby to hold him up. He was in! He felt dazed. Now he was delivered from his enemy, his tyrannical stepfather.

He studied the papers uneasily. What if Mr. Thrace disapproved of this enlistment? As a legal guardian, he could yank him out of the army, because Len was only twelve years old. He'd have the right, especially when it was discovered Len had lied about his age. Len didn't trust Mr. Thrace for one minute to consent. He'd interfere, sure as shooting!

Len must do a vanishing act. In two days' time he was due in Boston. A day or so after that, he'd be on his way to the battlegrounds. He dug through his desk, rounding up all the money he had on hand. He examined his possessions—his books, his tools, his collections of shells, rocks, and birds' nests, the set of animals he was carving, his clothes. He'd have to abandon everything except what he could carry in his pockets. He selected a small piece of fine walnut for carving and a whetstone for his knife. He'd wear what he had on; he'd leave without a good-bye.

It would be hard on his mother. He hated to think of that. Edie would raise a ruckus, too, she was so used to seeing him around. The Old Bean wouldn't care, but could be counted on to interfere, unless Len made his getaway very quietly and left no trace.

When he was once safe in the great Army of the North, he could perhaps let them know. He'd tell Mr. Thrace flatly that he wanted no further supervision or interference. "Consider me as good as dead," he would say in the letter he would write, when he felt it was safe to do so.

To give his mother a little comfort, he wrote a note. "Dear Mamma—I feel I have to leave home. Do not be unhappy. I love you, Mamma." He shrugged, regretful that he could not tell her why he "felt" he must leave or where he was going. He didn't dare. He must leave no clue, no trail.

He'd skip out right away. Then a glance outside told him this was a poor idea. It was still an hour before suppertime. Not that that mattered, when something so important was ahead of him—he shouldn't put his stomach first—but if he left now, he'd be missed within an hour. The family would start to fuss, then hunt. They'd go inquiring to neighbors. They'd listen for him to come in. After they went to bed, they'd sleep lightly and be watchful. Someone who knew him might see him on the road, mention it, and give away his route. Daylight wasn't good anyway, even though this day was dull and gray and muggy. A rainstorm was building up, he thought, and was glad, for it would get dark quicker and he could go sooner.

He sniffed. Something mighty good was being cooked downstairs. A chicken? Something spicy, too. Cake? Pudding? It wouldn't hurt to leave with a nice nourishing meal inside him. That reminded him that he ought to snag a little food to take with him. Otherwise, he might have to go a long time without it.

He galloped to the kitchen and took up a strategic position on a stool at the table, as he sometimes did before meals when he was extra famished. He grabbed a doughnut off a plate.

"You put that back," Edie said promptly. "You'll spoil your supper. You know what your mamma says."

"Aw, Edie!"

"Put it back," she ordered, but she smiled, as if she didn't care one way or another.

He pulled out his handkerchief and wrapped up the doughnut. "I'll eat it after supper."

"Oh, all right," she answered. "Only I don't see how you're going to find room inside."

He looked around the kitchen, locating some of the food to seize later when no one was around.

"It's so tarnation hot," Edie said, wiping her forehead with her hand. "And I've had to keep the oven going. Tonight I'll be up all hours, trying to catch up with the ironing."

He made a face. Edie ironed in the kitchen.

"You'll have to fetch in some wood, or I won't be able to heat the irons."

He jumped up. "I'll get it now," he said, and hustled out of the room, thinking how lucky it was he'd found out about the wood. Sure as mud, Edie would have shouted for him all over the place that evening to bring in wood, and then everyone would have known he was gone.

He brought in several loads, enough to keep her quiet, even if she ironed all night.

He felt nervous during supper. His appetite seemed to have disappeared. He had to force himself to eat, for he knew he must behave as he usually did at table. He almost overdid it by being extra polite, passing things promptly and without being asked, and studiously saying "sir" to Mr. Thrace.

He noticed his stepfather staring at him with what seemed to be an expression full of curiosity. Len smiled weakly.

"Well, well, well!" said Mr. Thrace. "I guess we're in a good mood tonight."

"Yes, sir," Len replied, feeling quite otherwise.

"How about a game of checkers?" Mr. Thrace suggested, in the jolly, resonant voice he had, which seemed so odd in a tyrant.

Checkers! They were almost never on friendly

enough terms to play games. Why did the Old Bean
have to suggest checkers on this night of nights?
He felt like screaming. "Er—er—I don't know," he
answered carefully.

"Oh, come on. We haven't tried a game for a long
time."

Len felt his heart sink to his boots. A game would
delay him at least an hour, maybe two. "It's—it's too
hot." He realized he didn't dare object too much.

"Nonsense! A game'll help us forget the heat.
What else did you plan to do with your evening?"

This question was a little too pointed for comfort.
Len tried not to show the panic in his thoughts. "Just
go to bed, I guess," he mumbled.

"I'll watch you," said his mother, smiling happily,
as if she thought their playing a game of checkers
showed that her son and his stepfather were at last
drawn close in the bonds of friendship.

Len cringed inside, thinking of the note he'd
written, which she'd discover in the morning when
he—if no more delays came up—would be miles
away. She had wept hard over Will's enlistment. He
felt terrible about how sad she'd feel tomorrow.

He wasn't able to retire to his room until ten

o'clock that evening, then had to wait cautiously, listening to every sound, until his folks had settled down for the night and the quiet indicated they'd gone to sleep.

He could hear the thump of Edie's iron off in the distant kitchen, and he sighed. He wouldn't be able to supply himself with food. All he had was the lone doughnut, greasing up his pocket through the handkerchief.

Sounds carried so through the house that he hardly knew how he was to get away. When he crossed his room, boards creaked, snapped, and popped. His door squeaked. The veranda route was closed to him, because it crackled with sounds of its own, easily recognizable. Going to the window, he peered out at the lowering sky, and saw a flash of lightning. It was going to storm hard. Maybe it would thunder.

At that instant a loud boom of it banged at him, almost as if he'd conjured it up. He grinned gleefully. Good old thunder. It would save him. Although it might waken his mother and stepfather, he doubted if they would get up. The thunder would cover any sounds he'd make. He was free.

Stealthily opening his door again, he stole along

the hall and down the stairs to reach the outer door, which he shut soundlessly behind him. With delight, he dashed out into the pouring rain, feeling it wash over him as if to wash away all that tied him to home. He started down the empty street on a run.

He hadn't had time to plan his journey, but felt he must put as much distance between him and Shrewsbury as he could that night. He splashed along enthusiastically, growing wetter and wetter, and not caring. The houses were darkened blobs among the trees, the church a pale ghostly sheath of white, with its steeple pointing up into the crackling sky.

When he neared the field where the recruitment tents had been set up, he slowed down, stuck his nose in the air, and walked past arrogantly. He'd like to see those men laugh at him now. He was as good as they were. And that general! Len could show him his army papers, signed by Judge Leonias Bradford, one of the chief recruitment officers of the Union. That would teach him to be scornful of Len.

Some of the tent flaps were rolled up to let in the cool air the rain had brought. Under the lantern light he saw groups of soldiers, sitting around playing cards, talking, eating. Soon he'd be in such a group, having a good time.

He sped on through the darkness.

It wasn't long before he began to wish he had a horse to ride. He couldn't run any longer, or even walk fast. The country road he had reached was rutted and hard to follow. The rain was so heavy that he couldn't see. Twice he took a wrong turn, although he knew the roads well near home. What would he do if he got to an area he didn't know, with its labyrinth of roads going in every direction? Some roads weren't marked. There was no one to ask, and he wouldn't dare inquire even if there was. No one must see him. Not until he was miles and miles away.

He plodded on for another hour. Each foot seemed to come up with a ton of mud on it. It fair wore him out just to lift his feet. He'd better find a place for a brief rest, or he'd collapse.

He watched for a barn near the road, and turned off into a farmyard with a stable and several sheds. The farmhouse nearby was dark. The rain softened the crunching and stamping noises made by the animals in the barn. He couldn't tell if cows or horses were

inside, not that it mattered. All he wanted was to
grope his way in and climb up into the loft full of
fragrant, dry hay. How good a few minutes' sleep
would feel!

He had barely pushed the door open a crack when
a thousand squawks rose around him. Wings flapped.
There were hisses, honkings. Something rose up and
pecked his shoulder. Something else bit him on the
leg. Just his luck! He'd aroused a gaggle of geese
inside.

That was not all. A man's voice roared over the
ruckus. "Get out of here, you hoss thief!"

The man leaped at him out of a stall, where he'd
been bedded down. He seized Len and poked a gun
into his ribs, then pushed him against the wall and
held him there.

Len heard a shout from outside. A second man appeared, carrying a lantern.

"I swan! It's a young un!" the first man said, gaz-
ing down at Len in astonishment. "Jeb, look what I
caught!"

Jeb pushed the lantern into Len's face. "What you
doing here?"

"Nothing."

"You aiming to steal a hoss?"

"No."

"Then why you creeping in here in the dead of night? Who's with you?"

"No one."

"You're lying! Hank," he went on, "shove the geese outside. If anyone's with him, they'll find him. Them geese are better watchdogs than dogs." He kept a grip on Len's shoulder until Hank had shooed the geese out and closed the door.

The men listened for sounds outside, then turned to Len when all remained quiet. "I'm alone. I came in to sleep," Len said sulkily.

They both stared at Len without moving. "Where you from?" Hank said then.

Len did not answer. That was the last thing he wanted to tell.

"Best look him over. Bet anything the kid's a runaway," Jeb said.

Len tried to dodge out from under their hands, but they were too quick for him. In a second they had him flat on the floor, and were jerking off his wet clothes. They found his army papers, which he'd wrapped up in waxed cloth, the only dry thing about him.

"Due in Boston day after tomorrow," said Jeb, after glancing through the document. "Maybe you was after a hoss at that. 'Fraid you wouldn't make it in time."

"No!" Len shouted.

"Looky here!" Jeb cried in sudden excitement. "The judge has signed this kid's papers."

They suddenly stood him on his feet. Hank slapped his shoulder. "All right, kid. Put on your clothes." He wrung out Len's shirt and handed it to him. "We had dealings with the judge last year. A lawsuit. He won our case for us. So if he's a friend of yours, you're all right."

"But what you doing walking to Boston in the middle of the night?" Jeb demanded.

Len did not reply. The two men exchanged glances.

"There's something fishy here for sure. Why ain't your folks helping you? You should be on the stage, traveling by day. This ain't right," Hank said.

Len was now dressed and his papers back inside

his shirt. He made a jump for the door. Again they grabbed him.

"No, you don't!" Jeb said. "Not till we say so. If you don't want to speak up, we'll not press you. Maybe it's none of our business, but we can't help but feel curious, see?"

"We had to set up night watch for hoss thieves, 'count of losing a hoss to them last week," Hank explained. "Stolen hosses are being sold to the army as fast as thieves can collar them. No animal's safe in his stable or pasture these days. That's why we was quick to misjudge you, coming in here at night."

"Let me go!" Len muttered.

He hardly knew what to think about these men. Maybe he could trust them, but he wasn't sure. He decided he'd better not confide in them at all.

"You've got a long walk ahead," Jeb said, "even though you've made good time from Shrewsbury."

Shrewsbury! How did they know? Then he realized the name was in his papers. He sighed. These were smart, observant men. Already they'd said he might be running away. Jeb had now guessed that he'd started his journey from home that night. They had found out too much about him for comfort.

Jeb said, "We could use this young fellow, Hank. What say he ride with us tomorrow when we take our animals in?"

"I'm willing," Hank answered.

They then explained that they were due to deliver ten horses of their own stock to a cavalry division near Boston. Len could ride with them and help with the animals.

He could hardly believe his good luck. He would easily arrive at Army Headquarters on time. What was even better, he was no longer in danger of being noticed, trudging along the road alone. If his folks started a hunt for him, they'd find no trace at all. In addition, he'd have a long happy ride, instead of miles of dreary walking.

Hank took him to the house and gave him milk to drink and a huge bone, well covered with meat, plus a piece of pie. With a dry nightshirt, which Hank handed him, he returned to the barn and crawled into the loft to sleep until dawn.

# 6 THE NEW RECRUIT

The ride was uneventful. Len said good-bye to the brothers at the outskirts of Boston and went down the pike on foot, feeling refreshed and easy in his mind.

He found it very simple to enroll at Army Headquarters with the proper papers to show. No questions were raised, no remarks made. A lieutenant stamped his papers and told him to go by horsecar to the station, where he'd take a train for New York. Len did not even see a general. At headquarters they

were rushing to get the new recruits off to Virginia
as speedily as possible. He saw that there would be
little danger in all the scramble that he would be held
back in case Mr. Thrace had guessed where he'd gone
and had telegraphed orders to stop him. All was confusion and bustle. He was a small, unnoticed recruit
among hundreds.

He enjoyed the long ride by horsecar, his first in
a conveyance of that type. It rattled so slowly over
the Boston cobblestones that he was able to examine
every building and monument and to study the famous harbor. Then came his first train ride, the cars
stuffed with recruits like himself. He was delighted
with every toot of the engine, with the grinding of
the wheels, with the bumps and jolts, and even with
the smoke that poured over the passengers through
the open windows, leaving each face black with soot.

In New York Len and his companions marched
from the railroad to the wharves. Len was thrilled
when he saw crowds of women and children lining
the street, watching them go by. They cheered and
waved flags, and made him feel prouder than ever
to be a soldier. The children threw flowers at the
men. Some of the women ran along beside the troops

and pushed offerings of food into the recruits' pockets. He found cheese, pickles, cookies, and fruit poked into his own.

From New York the recruits were piled into a steamer, which went gingerly along the coast, with everyone on the watch for trouble. The Rebs had shelled two boats in the past month, sinking one of them. Len stood on deck, with the wind combing his hair and his eyes scanning the white-capped waves, eager to be the first to spot a Reb ship, if there was any.

He was almost sorry to have the journey by steamer end, and to be disembarked and marched off to his final destination, the military base camp near Fairfax, Virginia, where he'd undergo training.

When he passed through Washington, it was full of troops, with Union encampments all around it. As he traveled, Len got the feeling that the terrible defeat at Bull Run had whetted interest in the war and sharpened the determination to win. The Rebs would have a hard time from now on, he felt, but they had a tremendous foothold. He was horrified to discover how strong the South was.

Fairfax was not many miles distant from Bull Run.

Len landed in the camp all agog to lay his hands on a musket and depart for a battleground. He forgot that he was to be a musician, and would have duties quite different from those of the regulation soldier.

The officer who checked his papers sent him to a tent to strip off his civilian clothes. The tent was crammed with new recruits, men of all ages and a few boys, who appeared to be from sixteen to eighteen years old. To his dismay, Len discovered that he was the shortest, thinnest, and youngest of the lot.

"Hey! Look at this goober!" cried a big brawny man, about thirty years old.

"Son," another said, "when you step up for your uniform, be sure to ask for the romper ration. That's 'cause they won't have a pair of pants in the whole army that'll fit you." The man laughed at his joke.

Len drew his lips tight and pretended not to hear. He didn't care much for being called a goober. A peanut. Indeed!

The quartermaster riffled through his sheaf of papers, handed one out to a young orderly, and signaled Len off to the side.

"Over here," said the orderly. Len looked at him with interest. He appeared to be about sixteen. The orderly said, "You're in the drum corps, ain't you? So'm I. They call me Crawfish." From a pile of clothing he hauled out a pair of blue trousers of lightweight wool and a jacket with red trimming and brass buttons. "This should be it." He squinted at Len, as if measuring him. "Choose yourself a cap."

Excitedly Len climbed into the outfit. It was very loose on him. He cinched up the trousers with a belt and took a big tack in the new galluses he'd bought. With the jacket on top, the trousers wouldn't look too bad, he hoped. Unfortunately, he floated inside the jacket. Even if he moved the buttons over, it would still be too large.

He caught some of the men eyeing him in amusement, and he scowled. It was the same old problem. He'd have to grow ten inches in the next month to look halfway decent.

"Don't accept the first thing you get," a man beside him said. "I think I can help you, maybe." Len looked up into a long, gaunt face. "My name's Putnam." The tall man held out a hand. "Fellow soldier."

Len felt his hand grasped for a minute in a firm, friendly clasp.

"That jacket won t do a-tall. The pants are terrible. I'm a tailor by trade. I'm going to poke into that pile and see if I can't dredge you up something better. You won't look so undersized if your duds come somewhere near fitting."

As Mr. Putnam reached for a jacket, Crawfish, the orderly, waved him away. "Don't bust in here and mix things up!"

Without a word, Mr. Putnam crossed over to the quartermaster. "How about letting me fit out your drum corps yonder?" he asked. "I'm a tailor, so I could fix you a right smart-looking corps."

In the another minute he came back and addressed the young orderly. "Are you in the drum corps?"

"Yup."

"Then take off that jacket. It's two sizes too big. You don't know how to judge carcasses. Look what you did to this fellow, giving him a tent to put on." He winked at Len.

In no time at all he had Crawfish reclothed, and Len into a smaller uniform. "It's still too big," Mr. Putnam said, "but I'll get permission to cut it down a little, leaving room for you to grow. You're just at the point where you'll shoot up fast, and fill out, too."

Len smiled gratefully at the man.

"Go outside for the rest of your gear," Mr. Putnam said. "Then hunt me up. Maybe we can set up our tents together after I finish this detail in here."

"Fine," Len said. "And thanks."

He wasn't sure he wanted to camp, or whatever one did, near this friendly man. He was old—old enough to be Len's father, around forty probably. Len thought he'd rather locate a few younger fellows, like Crawfish, the orderly. He'd noticed other boys in the crowd, too, probably all drum corps. He'd heard that most of the twenty chaps who would be in the drum corps were younger men. Someone fifteen or sixteen would suit him to camp with better than Mr. Putnam.

Before long he was equipped with a blanket, which he didn't appreciate, for it was frightfully hot this August day; shoes that were large but not uncomfortable; three pairs of sox; a change of underclothing; a piece of white-cotton drill, measuring some five by five feet; a knapsack; and a drummer sword. This last made him swell with pride, although it looked useless as a weapon. Food rations would be given later, he was told.

"How about a drum?" he asked.

"That's what they all ask." The officer he'd addressed tried to imitate Len's soprano. "Where's my bugle? I want my drum! Wait, young man! You'll be let know. Now skip!"

Len was dripping with perspiration in his wool suit. He removed his jacket to cool off. The new recruits were beginning to stake out places for their tents. Len's strip of canvas was only half a tent. He'd have to combine with someone else, and button his piece into the button holes of the second piece.

He watched two men put up their tent with forked sticks. They stuck the sticks into the ground six feet apart and laid a pole from one fork to the other. Then they joined their two pieces of drill, hung them over the center pole, and fastened them to the ground with small stakes. Len was soon busy hunting forked sticks. So was everyone else. The woods in which the camp lay became a shambles, as the men cut down the small shade-giving trees. The hot sun made the air shimmer. A heavy moistness seemed to drag at the men like a weight of lead. They moved wearily, steaming with sweat.

Len soon wilted. He drank his canteen dry several times, and still could not slake his thirst. "Wait till we're marching somewhere," he heard one of the men say. "Then we'll really parch!"

Len put his forked sticks over his shoulder, and set off to look for a tent companion. Many tents were up by now, with soldiers lounging by them waiting for further orders.

Jake Cooney, the brawny recruit who had noticed Len before, yelled, "Here's that goober again!" Everyone turned for a look.

A voice shouted, "Hey, Goober!"

Len glanced toward the person calling and saw a boy, in a drummer-corps uniform, beckoning. He hurried over to him.

"Knows his name already," Jake Cooney declared, and got a laugh.

Len didn't care. He saw a prospective comrade in the boy who had called.

"Got a tentmate, Goober?" the boy asked.

"Nope." Len noticed the name, Bill Harrison, neatly lettered on the boy's knapsack. "Where'd you get that? It's not army issue."

"An old great-aunt gave it to me, all lettered. I'm keeping it, 'cause it has more pockets than the army one."

They walked off together, watching for a place to pitch their tent. Bill said he came from Camden, New Jersey. He was sixteen. His parents had made no objection to his enlisting. He had four brothers and sisters, plus numerous uncles, aunts, and cousins. His knapsack was full of cookies, preserved meats, jams, and pickles from home. He carried his civilian clothes and other personal possessions in a bundle under his arm.

"We'd better get up our energy by eating some of this," Bill remarked. So after they had scraped the ground clear for their tent, they opened Bill's preserves. Before they had raised a mouthful, they were surrounded by soldiers.

"Spare me a crumb!" one bawled.

Others cried, "Me, I'm starved!" "Ain't et nothing for a hour!" "The heat's got me!" "I need food."

The men edged in, reaching out, clowning, laughing. To get even a cookie, both boys had to grab. Len swiftly snared a jar of homemade corned beef, and sat on it. Into his pockets he crammed all the cookies he could snatch. Bill managed to hang on to a jar of preserved cherries.

"Well, what do you know!" Bill exclaimed a few seconds later. The men had faded away magically, now that there wasn't a scrap of food left. "We should have set up our tent first," he added, "and done our eating inside on the quiet. Did you make off with anything at all, Goober?"

Len patted his pockets. "Sure, but we'd better pitch tent now, so we don't raise another raid."

The ground was too soggy to support the poles. They cut extra stakes for props, got the crosspiece up and the white drill over; then they crawled inside and feasted, although with caution and with many glances outside to make sure no one was noticing that they still had food. When everything was gone, they crawled back outside and fanned themselves with their shoes. Len felt dizzy in the heat.

"Let's hunt for a brook to dunk in," he proposed.

"We're supposed to stay in camp, ain't we?"

"What for? We aren't doing anything. Let's go."

They got up wearily. Even with their jackets off, they were steaming. They left their gear and shoes piled up inside their tent and walked barefoot through camp. All the tents were up now, in scattered clusters where the ground was best. The white shelters seemed to cover several acres.

"This must be a big company," Len remarked. "Never saw so many tents in my life."

"It must have rained a lot lately," Bill said, "there's so many puddles." They waded into them, hoping to cool their feet, but even the water was hot.

At that moment they heard a bugle call.

# 7        MR. PUTNAM

Some of the men in camp put on jackets and caps, and headed at once for the big tents where they'd been mustered in. Others stood and stared. These were the new recruits, and they didn't know what to do. Then came shouted orders. The two boys scampered back for their discarded jackets, caps, and shoes.

"I guess it's summons for drill," Bill said.

Men were lining up in fours when they reached the parade ground. Len got into line beside Bill and stood as straight and tall as he could, although the muggy heat made him long to lie down. So much sweat rolled into his eyes, he could hardly see.

"Attention!" the sergeant bawled.

The lagging lines of men pulled themselves erect. "Forward march!"

They tramped to the end of the camp, then back. Len tried to use the knowledge of marching he had acquired from watching the parades at home. He felt as if the drums beat for him alone.

The lines went back and forth a number of times; then, as the men waited hopefully for dismissal, the officer in charge shouted, "Strike tents!"

Men near Len groaned.

"What's it mean?" Len asked.

It didn't take long to find out. In a second the company was in a turmoil. Men yanked up stakes and forked sticks, undoing all that they had so laboriously set up. Len and Bill unbuttoned their cotton drill, folded the pieces, jammed things into their knapsacks. Then, as drums rolled, veteran corps men, new recruits, and the two boys ran back to the lines with their knapsacks on their backs. Len and Bill had taken fifteen minutes. The officer in charge told the company everyone should have got his tent down in two minutes, with five at the most to get back into position.

Next the raw recruits began a march cross-country, following a road full of sticky Virginia mud and water-filled ruts into which their feet sank ankle deep. Their new shoes filled with slime.

We must be going to attack the enemy, Len thought excitedly, pleased that on his first day in army camp he was getting into a battle.

He wasn't, however. The men tramped four miles, while their officers tried to stir them on to something that could be called marching. Then they were ordered back to camp, and reached the original site in the late afternoon, panting under the heat and with their feet hurting in the new army shoes.

The men were fed; then they had to pitch their tents all over again.

"Why'd we have to go all that way for nothing?" Len asked, disappointed that there had been no sign of battle or of a lurking enemy.

No one was able to answer.

Evidently the men were off duty until further orders. Len wandered about, and came upon Mr. Putnam under a tree, busily darning a sock. He had forgotten the man. He nodded to him, and was going to walk on, when Mr. Putnam said, "Hope your shoes fit better'n mine."

"Mine are loose."

"They rubbing any?"

"Don't know."

"Guess they aren't or you'd be hollering. My shoes sliced several holes in my brand-new sox during that march." He threaded a needle expertly and went on darning. Len dropped down onto the grass beside him and idly examined fragments of wood that had fallen there. One piece looked possible for whittling, and he got out his knife.

"How do you like army life?" Mr. Putnam asked.

"So far so good," Len said with a shrug. He felt a little bored actually.

"I notice you found a tentmate."

"Yup."

"You can keep each other from getting homesick."

"There's no danger," Len said.

"Well, maybe not. Have you been away from home before?"

"Nope." He tried to keep the scorn out of his

voice, for privately he thought homesickness was a sissy feeling to have.

"Sometimes it hits you unexpected like—say, when there's not much going on, or you're alone on duty somewhere and it's dark and raining. Sometimes you're among so many new people you feel as if you haven't a friend in the world, and you feel lonesome. Then's when you can get awful homesick."

"I won't," Len said resolutely. "I like it here."

"Lucky boy. I think maybe I have a touch of it."

Len glanced at the man indifferently, then was caught by the worried look on his face.

"The trouble with me is," Mr. Putnam went on, "I'm wondering if I did right to enlist. I didn't need to. My wife's not very strong, and the boy, Dick, is only ten; my little girl, Lucy, only four. I'm in for three years."

"Me too," said Len.

"When I signed up I thought the war would be over in less than a year perhaps. I don't mind a year, but now that I'm down here and have looked around and heard some of the talk, I'm afraid we're in for a long war. The Rebs are farther ahead than I thought. We're in for a bad time, Son."

Len scowled. He didn't like the man's gloomy remarks.

"I miss my family. It beats all how I miss them,
especially since I came to realize what I've let them
in for. What's my wife going to do if I'm wounded?"

Len got to his feet. If Mr. Putnam was going to
be so droopy, he wanted to leave him. The war was
glorious, with its floating banners and rat-a-tat of
drums and the quick smack of marching feet on stony
streets. He fingered the sword hanging at his side.

Mr. Putnam glanced at it. "How do you think
you'll make out with that toad-sticker?"

Len's glance turned angry.

"Oh now, that was stupid of me. Forget it, boy.
I don't know what's ailing me tonight. The truth is,
your sword really isn't much good—just a decora-
tion. Don't know why the army issues it to the band
corps. It's purely for looks. Sit down again, and let's
see if we can hit it off somehow. Where do you live?"

"Shrewsbury, Massachusetts."

"I'm from Germantown, Pennsylvania. Is your
father in this, too?"

"I have a stepfather. He's home."

"I see." Mr. Putnam looked at him shrewdly.

"Which explains why a boy only twelve years old has entered the army."

"I'm fifteen," said Len.

"Twelve," Mr. Putnam answered. "I know bones, and I know sizes, and I know boys, and I haven't cut cloth for twenty years without learning to tell ages. But I won't say anything—not a word. You're a bit like my boy, Dick. I took to you at once. Well, that's the way it goes. I guess I've messed things up now, so you won't speak to me next time you see me."

He looked rueful. Len's annoyance with him melted. "Aw, I'm not like that," he said.

"What do you play in the band?"

"I think they'll give me a drum."

"Drum, eh? I was hoping you'd say fife. I play the fife at home myself. Pleasant little instrument." He shook out the stone he was using as a darning egg. "Let's go down to the hollow yonder. I see some fellows starting card games. Do you play pinochle?"

# 8       THE DRUM CORPS

The next day army life settled into a pattern, at least as far as camp was concerned. Len and Bill were separated from the main body of recruits and put with the drum corps for training and drilling. The drum-corps major, a man named Jeffers, tried out the twelve new boys who had come into the regiment, and picked some for the bugle, others for drum or fife.

Len happily rubbed his drumsticks, and tried a surreptitious tapping against a tree.

Lessons started. The drummers had to learn rhythms that would show men in battle where to go during the advances or retreats. The drummers must also beat tattoo for evening roll call, know the long roll and the double and single drag, and be able to imitate the sound of musketry. It wasn't much like the sort of drumming that accompanied the marching tunes Len had heard in the parades.

There were hours of practice every day after guard-mounting exercises and between countless battalion drills. The drum corps had to keep their uniforms spotless, the brass buttons shined and buttoned regardless of August heat, the caps at a set angle, the swords hung just so, and the instruments protected from misuse.

The hot weather continued. Rain fell frequently. Some days the whole camp was a sea of red mud. Len and Bill dragged branches into their shelter tent to keep themselves off the wet ground. Water seeped through the cotton drill and drizzled down over them as they tried to sleep. It seemed to them that the bugler called them out every morning long before they'd had their quota of rest.

Everyone in camp was in the same situation.

Len thought sometimes of his comfortable room at home and of the good food that Edie brought to the table, although he didn't wish to be there at present. This was different. One couldn't expect the comfort one got at home, and it was lots of fun being with men of all ages and with the younger fellows in the drum corps. He liked eating in camp, free to lick his fingers and sprawl on the ground. But he wished the food was better. The meat was greasy. There was a lot of hardtack. He passed up these tasteless biscuits, which nearly broke his teeth, and filled his plate generously with everything else. He had to grow. To grow, he must eat. He didn't want to be called Goober all his life. Even Mr. Putnam had discovered his nickname and called him that at times.

One day Len ran across Jake Cooney, the brawny young man who had first called him Goober. "Hey, Goober. Have you heard what them Confeds are singing about you?"

"Nope, what's that?" Len readied himself for teasing.

Jake sang gaily, " 'Just before the battle the General hears a row'—That's the Confed general, you

understand—'He says, "The Yanks are coming"'
—That's us—' "I hear their rifles now." He turns
around in wonder, and what do you think he sees?
The Geor-gi-a militia eating goober peas!'"

Soldiers nearby laughed. Len grinned gamely.
That would be a good song to send home sometime
when he wrote his mother. It would help fill a page
and give her a laugh, too. He decided not to tell her
that Goober was his nickname.

It seemed to Len that army life made everyone
fidgety. The men wriggled and wriggled inside their
uniforms, and they scratched themselves incessantly.
He felt himself begin to itch, first here, then there,
and blamed it on skin rashes from the insufferable
heat.

One day as he sat in his shirt sleeves, playing
checkers with Mr. Putnam, he saw a little white
thing creep over his wrist—an insect. He started to
brush it off and then discovered a whole chain of
them crawling along. Wherever they went, he felt
himself itch madly.

"What's that?" he demanded, picking the creatures off and squashing them between his fingers.

"So they finally got you," Mr. Putnam said. "They got me the second day. It's lice, Son."

Lice! Len looked at his arm with a shudder. He was really shocked. He'd always associated lice with filth, feeling that people who had such bugs on their bodies were extra dirty, did not take decent care of themselves, and were even rather low on the human scale. People from his sort of world didn't have lice. He knew he was much dirtier than he had ever been in his life, due to the mud, dust, and the poor washing and laundering facilities in the camp, but to be so filthy he'd taken on lice appalled him.

"The whole army's got them," Mr. Putnam said.

"Everybody?"

"Yes-sir-ee—even the colonels and generals. Not a man here's but got them."

Len felt better, less disgraced.

"Doggone!" he exclaimed, and opened his shirt to look at suspicious itchy places. "They're all over me!"

"You can wash everything you've got on and yourself, to boot, but in five minutes your little friends will be right back," said Mr. Putnam.

Len retreated to the edge of camp and there, hidden a little by some bushes, tried to rid his clothes of the lice. He could not stand doing this out among the others, with the men joking about it. Most of them sat out in the open, doing their "nitting," as they called it.

Len thought of his mother. She should be around now. Wouldn't she have a fit!

Back at the tent he asked Bill how he fared.

"Lice don't like me," Bill answered. "They just walk across me and go to someone else."

"To me," Len said gloomily.

"Got them bad, Goober?"

"Yes."

"Maybe you should rub on some kerosene. That should stink them out."

"And where would I get kerosene? There's none in camp, except in the officers' lanterns."

"Try the sutler. He's in camp today."

Len didn't know what a sutler was. He'd discovered that every time he showed ignorance about something, Bill said, "You poor idiot, ain't you heard of that? Where you been?"

This usually annoyed Len, so now he pretended

he knew all about sutlers, and set off. "Not that way, Goob!"

Len shrugged, and continued stubbornly in the wrong direction, feeling cross with himself for being so touchy. He guessed it was finding those bugs that made him feel cranky.

He saw Mr. Putnam coming. "I've just been shopping at the sutler's," he said. "Got you a sewing outfit. Reckon you'll need it when your buttons start snapping off and your sox give out."

"Why—th-thanks." Len stared in amazement at the package of needles and thread. Imagine *him* using it. Him sewing! He'd never mended in his life. He hadn't planned to. But he saw he'd have to; if he didn't, his uniform might not pass Major Jeffers' rigorous inspections. Then he'd be in trouble.

Mr. Putnam was grinning at him, as if he knew what Len thought about sewing for himself. "The sutler's got a salve that relieves itching," he added. "Got you some." And he handed out a second package.

"Sa-a-ay—you shouldn't bother about—about— uh—thanks!" Len felt embarrassed by the man's kind attention.

"I miss doing things for my kids," Mr. Putnam said in explanation. He shifted his gaze from Len's and walked off, his shoulders a little hunched. He looked tired and sad.

Len noticed a covered wagon, surrounded by soldiers. That must be the sutler, a peddler who sold stuff and went from camp to camp. He hurried over to examine the load of boxes, bottles, and cans. There were bags of flour, tobacco, playing cards, stationery, coffee, condensed milk, cheese, sox, knives, newspapers, pies, and cakes. A whiskery man with crafty eyes was selling them.

Jake Cooney was in the crowd, and raised a laugh by yelling, "Goober's buying kerosene. I wonder why."

Len smiled wryly and picked up a fruit pie. It cost two dollars, which he thought was an outrageous price. But he kept it. He was starving for something fruity and sweet. For days now he'd been on hardtack, starchy food, and greasy meat. However, when he sampled the pie, he was disappointed. It was soggy, undercooked. He threw most of it away and sighed, thinking of Edie's and his mother's flaky crusts and succulent fillings.

\*

The first mail arrived in camp.

Len had cautiously written his mother that he had joined the army, and not to worry, for he was happy and felt himself to be much needed. This last was a hint to her to let him alone. It was also a hint for Mr. Thrace.

Len felt uneasy when he found a letter from his stepfather. Inside it was a ten-dollar bill. The letter said, "Dear Boy, I hear that army pay doesn't always come through on time. I wouldn't like you to feel short when you want a few luxuries, so am enclosing a ten-dollar bill to use for your pleasure. Yours, Archibald Thrace."

Ten dollars? That was a large sum. Mr. Thrace was being extremely generous. Why? Len read the letter again. It was formal. The man was keeping his distance. He put no strings on Len or on his use of the money. It was evidently a gift, and the man wanted him to have a good time with it. Len felt vastly uncomfortable. Was this a trick? Why didn't Mr. Thrace jump on him for running away? Why didn't he threaten to yank him out of the army? Maybe he felt it was useless. Len was *in*.

He hugged himself. That was it. He was *in!* He had put it over by getting Judge Leonias Bradford's backing. No old stepfather could get him out.

Mr. Thrace enclosed a letter from Will to Len's mother, telling that he'd been in an active war zone. He'd had to tend wounded on the battlefield. His closing item filled Len with envy. Will's unit was mounted, and he'd drawn a fine horse.

The last letter was from Emily Jane.

"Dear Len," she wrote. "My friends and I are most anxious to serve our noble soldiers during their time of tribulation, and think we should devote our best efforts to bringing cheer. So each one of us is going to adopt a soldier as a sort of pen companion. I have chosen you, and will write you faithfully and, perchance, send you small things that will contribute to your well-being and comfort. My father, Judge Leonias Bradford, has gone west on a recruiting tour, thus was unable to get in direct touch with you, as he planned, when you went through Washington. He was much pleased that you were taken into the army through his own personal intervention."

As Len finished reading his mail, Bill ran up to him breathlessly. "Goober!" he said. "Major's mad as a scorched cat today. Better watch your drumming!"

"Watch it!" Len yelled. "All I do is watch it! Blast it, anyway!"

"Well, he's out to get you. Crawfish told me."

"How's he know?"

"Ask him."

Apprehensively Len stalked along beside Bill to band practice. He felt discouraged. He wanted desperately to be a drummer, but he wasn't catching on in his use of the drumsticks. His timing was faulty. His fingers didn't seem to have the knack for the quick rhythms he must master. He'd practiced till he was gasping, only to have the major bawl, "Do you think the army's got bunions? How are they going to march to *that*, young man?"

Everyone played better than he. The boys had all made good progress. Only he still played off beat.

"Baldwin!" Major Jeffers roared almost immediately. "Turn in your instrument! Ask Captain Goodrich to find you another job."

Len looked at the officer, and his face paled with disappointment. He'd failed in what he wanted most to do—be in the band and go marching off at the head of the company, leading the way to battle. Now

what was to become of him? Being relegated to the
ranks of the infantry, one among thousands of foot
soldiers, was most unappealing to him, now that he'd
had a taste of being in the drum corps. Yet that was
all he could expect. He saw Bill look at him with
sympathy. So did some of the others.

The band boys were nearer his age, too. In the
regular army he'd be with older men, and they'd tease
and plague him for being young, or else be fatherly
and fuss over him and load him with unwanted
advice. They'd never put him on their level, as the
boys of the band did.

He saluted and walked off smartly, doing his best
not to show how crushed he felt. On his way to the
captain's tent he met Mr. Putnam.

"You're just the one I want to see," said Mr.
Putnam. "I thought you might like to add to your
musical skills, so I wrote my wife Martha to send me
my fife, so's I could turn it over to you. It was just
lying around there at home. Might as well be used."

"No!" Len shouted, and clenched his fists to keep
from screaming or letting tears burst out. To be
offered a fife now! That was more than he could
endure. He stood a second with his chest heaving,

then swung about to run, but Mr. Putnam seized his
arm and held him fast.

"What's the matter? What's happened, man?"

Being called "man" helped Len. He swallowed,
got himself under control, and muttered, "Major
Jeffers kicked me out of the band. My drumming's
no good."

Mr. Putnam was silent a minute, as if stunned by
the announcement. "What does the man expect in
just two weeks?" he demanded. "Len, had you played
anything before entering the army?"

"No."

"Had the others in the band?"

"I think most of them had."

"Well, that's a talking point."

"Not with that old turkey."

"Did you say anything?"

"Say anything! You don't say things to the officers!"

"Smart boy. You kept the ground clear. That's
fine. I can do something about this. I've noticed that
you pick up tunes easily. Your ear is good, I'd say.
Now if you could get yourself transferred from drum
to fife, I could coach you."

"Transferred!" Len exclaimed. "But I'm kicked out of the band entirely."

"An item. A detail." Mr. Putnam shrugged and drew up his eyebrows. "Let me talk to Major Jeffers. He needs a man like you around." He slapped Len's shoulder reassuringly. "Meanwhile, take this fife of mine and look it over." He put the package into Len's hands to unwrap. "Odd thing," he added. "My boy Dick seems to have mailed the fife. I wonder why Martha didn't. I suppose she was busy." Shaking off his slightly worried look, he watched Len pull out the instrument.

At the end of the day Major Jeffers sent for Len. "So you want to be a fifer."

"I want another chance, sir," Len said firmly.

"You're a runt," said the major, "and runts don't look good behind large drums. Think maybe your friend's right—you should be a fifer. Report for practice as usual, young man. Also, if your friend offers fife lessons, snap them up."

"Yes, *sir!*" Len said, so pleased he could hardly keep his feet on the ground as he stood before the major. He tried not to notice that the man put his hand over his mouth, hiding an amused grin.

Len sought out Mr. Putnam immediately. "Hurrah!" Mr. Putnam cried. He got out the fife and played a tune Len had never heard before. It was as gay as "Yankee Doodle," and made him think of people bouncing about in a barn dance.

"Where'd you learn that jig?"

"It's not a jig. It's a galop. But you weren't far off calling it a jig, for they both are dance tunes. You like it, I hope."

"Yup." Len whistled a bit of it. "What do you call it?"

"Hm! I never thought to name it. Probably should. Nowadays tunes have fancy names, like 'The Lark at Dawn' or 'The Maiden's Delight.'"

"Your tune's too nice for such silly names."

"Galop—galop. Hey, how about this for a name? 'The Goober Galop!'"

"Not Goober!" Despite his objection, Len felt his heart glow. He was sure Mr. Putnam was teasing him, but could not help feeling good at having his nickname linked with so pretty a tune, one composed by his friend.

"Goober suits it," Mr. Putnam said. "It's just a little penny-whistle tune, so it should have a penny-whistle name like yours. You wouldn't be insulted, would you?"

"No, for heaven's sake!"

"Then that's it. 'The Goober Galop.' Now let's get started with the fife."

As Len blew, Mr. Putnam's sad eyes lighted a little.

**9**                      **GENERAL GOOBER**

For a while after that camp life was pleasant, at least to Len, despite his itches and increasing dislike of army food. With Mr. Putnam's help, he caught on to fifing, and even made progress with drumming. However, he had to practice out of hearing of the major, to avoid making mistakes from nervousness.

There was only one thing missing—no fighting. He felt as if a lot of time was being wasted training recruits. Then he discovered that part of the huge company stationed in the camp melted away mysteriously one night and was not seen there again. They had gone to the battlefields, their training completed. New recruits appeared in their places. In about a month Len was practically a veteran, compared to the new men, yet had never been on a battleground or heard the sound of enemy musketry.

One day he was assigned to musketry drill, and went marching smartly past Mr. Putnam and Jake Cooney with a gun over his shoulder. "There goes General Goober," Jake said. "Bet he falls down."

Len grinned. He didn't care what Jake said anymore. The soldier had to have his fun, the poor ape. Someday Len would return some of his compliments and get a laugh out of the men at Jake's expense. Just wait!

Next came picket duty. Len felt as if he'd been living just for this. Now he was truly a part of the great war, not merely eternally drilling, marching, drumming, and playing a fife, while never braving danger. Picket duty meant possible contact with the enemy.

Len and three soldiers tramped off into the woods, with orders to march to a post seven miles from camp. "Are the Rebs drawing in on us, do you think?" he asked, trying to sound professional.

"Could be," Nat Jones answered. "They say things is moving on the Rappahannock."

"That isn't very near."

"Near enough. Anyways, from now on, we've got to be sharp. The Rebs have more guerrillas than is healthy 'round these parts."

That sounded good to Len. Maybe they'd have a skirmish tonight.

When they reached their post, Nat said, "I'll take the first watch. You come up at midnight, Black. Goob—I mean Baldwin—you take over about three A.M., and you, Hickman, can finish off." With that he walked over to a wood-covered hillslope and disappeared.

"I thought we all watched together," said Len.

His companions, men about Mr. Putnam's age, did not answer. Mr. Black was scratching the ground clear of leaves. Mr. Hickman was gathering stones. Len saw him set up a campfire and light it.

"Do we dast have a fire?" Len demanded. "Won't the Rebs see it?"

"It don't matter here. Look over yonder—up that rise. The Rebs have a fire, too. They're probably swilling down coffee already."

Sure enough, there was a thread of smoke up over the hill beyond them. Len felt bewildered. This was truly a queer war, where enemies gave their positions away to each other by building coffee fires.

As the smell of coffee rose from Mr. Hickman's pot, Len clawed into his ration pack for his cup and hardtack. Mr. Hickman poured. Len dunked his biscuit, glad for a chance to soften the wretched, tasteless stuff. As he lifted the piece to his mouth, he saw something move. A couple of worms were crawling out of it.

He dropped the biscuit like a hot poker. "Hey!" he cried.

"Weevils," Mr. Hickman remarked. "They always come out when you dip biscuit in coffee."

Len tore open the rest of his hardtack ration and examined it. "The whole thing's rotten with them! I can't eat that stuff!" He threw the package into the fire.

"Easy, man," said Mr. Hickman. "You're going to be mighty hungry, burning up your ration for two days. Except for the bit of dried meat, that's all you've got."

"But weevils!" Len exclaimed in horror.

"Yuh, I know." Mr. Hickman cautiously gnawed a corner of a biscuit. "I don't soak mine. I just sort of eat and hope there ain't any critters. 'Course, if the weevils is right bad, I give up—but I can't say I like going hungry, either."

Len examined his coffee suspiciously. It was clear. He drank it. He drew away from the fire, no longer hungry and feeling a little sick.

Mr. Black drew out a pack of cards. "I reckon we could play."

Mr. Hickman squatted down beside him, but Len felt too restless. "After a while," he muttered.

"You might collect a little wood while it's still light," Mr. Hickman suggested.

Len nodded.

"Remember the password, if you meet anyone," the man added.

Len walked off, glad for an excuse to look around. The sun had set, and twilight shadows were creeping down the hillslope. He walked softly, wondering if any Southern pickets were prowling through the woods as futilely as he seemed to be doing.

The trees opened upon a small clearing in a hollow. Here he found the ground strewn with rubbish.

He saw cloth scraps, which seemed to come from both clothing and shelter tents; broken cups; bent plates; ant-covered rations of pork; knives; papers that looked like torn-up letters; even a saber, lying half buried in dirt near blackened stones where a fire had burned.

He walked about, puzzled. Who had been here? Northern pickets or Rebs? He picked up a bit of frayed cloth and felt a prickle of excitement. It was gray. It must have come from a Confederate uniform.

He glanced about apprehensively, half expecting to see a Johnny Reb lurking among the trees. Near the saber was a large white stone, with a dark stain across it. He had never seen such a stain before, but he knew instinctively what it was. Blood!

Hesitantly he touched the stain. It was hard and dry. Someone had been wounded here quite recently, he was sure. The blood had dried in the heat, and it hadn't rained for two days to wash it away. This meant that any time in the last two days someone had been shot or knifed here. Had it been a Reb picket, wearing gray?

He wondered if Nat knew about this, and if it was his duty as picket to go notify the fellow. Or should he go to camp instead and tell the other two? He could ask their advice. They'd been on picket duty before and would know.

He started back. But now the light had changed considerably. He could hardly see among the trees. Everything looked different. Which way had he come? He'd wandered around the clearing, too, without noting just where he'd entered. He'd be in a fine pickle if he got lost in the woods while on picket duty. What if his turn came to be sentinel, and he didn't show up?

He took a few steps here, then there. No direction seemed right. The darkness grew deeper. Finally he remembered the coffee fire. In a jiffy he was scrambling up the nearest tall tree.

A sigh of relief tore out of his lungs. Hurrah! He saw the fire. He lined it up with a white birch below him. After passing the birch, if he wasn't sure, he could skin up another tree to get his sights.

Half an hour later he walked into camp with an armload of wood. "I've got news," he said, trying to sound like an old hand at reporting discoveries while on picket duty. "Somebody's had a skirmish back there."

"Yuh," Mr. Hickman grunted. "That was a couple of days ago. Nat Jones and me, we got the Rebs. Routed them, and drug one back as a prisoner."

"How many?" Len was so impressed he could hardly keep from stuttering.

"Six." Mr. Hickman scratched his ear and yawned. "You better turn in, chum, or you'll fall asleep at your post."

"Did you—did anyone get killed?" Len asked.

"One almost did," Mr. Hickman said, "but his comrades set him on his feet, and he took off. Reckon he's running yet."

"I saw blood," Len said.

Mr. Hickman and Mr. Black glanced at each other. The look they exchanged gave Len a feeling of being shut out suddenly. Mr. Hickman didn't look as if he was joking now. "That feller we hit got it in the arm. I don't think it was bad, just looked bad. Don't think about it, Son."

Mr. Black opened his knapsack. He lifted out a package of dried plums. "Have a few, lad; then go lie down."

"No, thanks," said Len. "I've got rations. Shouldn't take yours."

His pride was hurt. The two soldiers had tangled
with the enemy and had badly wounded a man only
two days ago, but they were softening up the event for
Len, as if they thought him too tender a soldier to
look at blood without flinching. They were treating
him like a girl, and now offered food to get his mind
off what he'd seen. Well, he'd show them! Just wait
until the enemy came prowling around tonight!

Mr. Black woke him and led him to a post on the
ridge above. Len was surprised to see spots of light
dotting the dark valley below. They were Reb campfires.

"The idea is to watch for any enemy movement,"
Mr. Black said. "They've got a sneaky system. They
keep a man or two feeding the fires while their regiment slips off. Keep your eyes open, and listen for all
you're worth. Twigs'll snap. Leaves'll crackle. Men'll
grunt or breathe heavy. In a still night you'll be surprised how a sound will carry. If you get evidence
that Johnny Reb's pulling out men, you come tip-
toeing down fast and quiet, hear?"

Len bristled with excitement. He slunk down on
the rock. Mosquitoes whined about his ears and
feasted where they liked on his exposed face. He did

not dare slap at them for fear he'd make a noise.

The night was hot and he was dying of thirst, but he had drunk his canteen dry and forgotten to refill it at the brook. He was hungry, too, but again, because he might make noise, he hesitated to open his canned meat ration. He'd have to learn to look after himself better than that, he thought, and tried to forget his discomfort by staring continuously down into the valley.

The fires twinkled at him. Sometimes he saw one flare up a little, as if new sticks had been thrown on. The silence was deep, and yet at times leaves rustled as a breeze touched them, insects churred, or a bird chirped drowsily. Nothing seemed to change. He felt anxious, fearing he'd failed to discover Rebs creeping off in the dark to launch an attack on a Union outpost. Yet he could detect no sign of movement at all.

Then something stirred somewhere below him on the slope. He couldn't tell what had caught his attention. It was neither the snapping of a twig nor the rustling of leaves. It was a sloshy sound, which lasted for only a few seconds and was very faint. Grasping his musket, he slunk softly toward it, then waited. Nothing more occurred, yet he felt uncomfortable.

Something had made that noise. Something was there!

He waited so long his leg went to sleep. He straightened it out, tried to rub back the circulation and to listen for all he was worth.

Finally he heard a crunch, crunch, crunch over dry leaves. Slowly and steadily someone was advancing, walking with soft footfalls, yet apparently indifferent to any noise he made.

Len set himself into position for firing, and cautioned himself to remember his instructions. He must demand the countersign and not fire at once. He'd been told that green rookies often lost their heads and killed needlessly. More than one raw soldier had shot one of his own comrades. The captain had said, "So hold your fire."

Len shivered with apprehension. Two days ago Mr. Hickman and Nat Jones had fought with six of the enemy just a short distance from this post. Sure as fate, a group of Rebs had found out he was here and were slipping up on him. Yet why did they pay so little attention to the noise they were making? Was it because there were dozens of them?

He slunk forward again, crouched behind a tree,

and stared down into the black grove. He saw a gray-ish shape moving, and called out, "Who goes there?"

A loud but mellow voice answered immediately. "Moo!" it said.

Up toward him came a cow.

A cow! He fell back in disgust. If that wasn't his luck! She mooed again loudly.

"Shut up!" he said angrily.

The stupid beast was making too much noise. She would give him away to the enemy, bellowing like that, mooing all over the place, and now crashing through the trees, hurrying to reach him.

"Go back!" he said.

But she came on, mooing again. She placed herself dumbly before him and mooed in his face.

"Hush up, you!" he ordered.

He dashed to his lookout rock, stared earnestly about to see if there was any sign of change below. Surely the Rebs must have heard that cow!

When he turned around again, the animal was directly behind him, her muzzle touching his shoulder. This was horrible. He'd have to urge her back. If he let her stay on the edge of the cliff, her voice would carry down to the enemy.

He pushed her, but she did not budge. "Plague take you!" he muttered wrathfully. She mooed again, and prodded him with her head, almost pushing him off the rock.

What was he to do?

He felt along her neck and discovered a rope knotted around it with an end dangling, but too short for tying her to a tree. At least he could lead her, so he grasped the rope and tugged. She moved with him docilely and, except for the noise made by her hooves, went quietly. He didn't know where to take her. He wondered if he should leave his post and rush her down to the the three soldiers to get her out of hearing of the valley.

As he pondered his next move, his hand on the cow's neck, he saw her turn her ears forward. Then she mooed again, the loudest moo of all.

"What in tarnation!" a voice exclaimed from the dark beyond. Nat Jones stepped out of the shadows. Immediately he doubled up on the ground, holding his sides, rolling about, choking back laughter. "Goober, you beat all!" he whispered, when he could finally control himself.

"What'll I do with this cow?" Len demanded.

"Sure now—milk her. That's what she wants. She's strayed from somewheres. There's several abandoned farms roundabout. Milk her."

"I don't know how. What's more, she makes more racket than a whole battalion!"

Nat had another spasm of laughing, but clipped it short to say, "True enough, Son. 'Twas her bawling fetched me up here. Thought it was a Reb signal. Didn't figger on finding breakfast rations instead, and furnished by a Confederate cow at that. I expect you're thirsty. Open up your canteen, so's I can squirt in some milk. Then I'll take the old girl off your hands. In another hour you come down for flapjacks. Hickman's due then to take over up here."

Next morning the tramp back to camp pained Len's feet. There were holes in all the sox he possessed, and those he wore did not protect him from the rubbing of the rough leather army shoes. He had thought darning too womanish a thing to do, although he'd seen that his friend Mr. Putnam mended his sox regularly. But then, Mr. Putnam was a tailor. Len hadn't yet used his sewing kit, and would have thrown it away if he hadn't realized that Mr. Putnam would be disappointed after having given it to him.

Now as he limped along the dusty road his feet hurt horribly. Desperate, he took off his shoes, and discovered that his toes and heels were covered with blisters, most of which had burst and were oozing. The raw flesh stung like fury.

Nat Jones looked over and shook his head. "You've got trouble, boy. You should mend your sox."

"I'll get new ones from the quartermaster."

"No, you won't. The army don't hand out sox for the asking. You got to make them last till next issue, and that's maybe in more than two months."

"The sutler has some."

"He's left. No telling when the next wagon'll show up."

"I'll get along somehow." Len tied the laces, slung his shoes over his shoulder, and hobbled along barefoot. This felt better.

They were taking the cow with them, but she slowed them up. Finally Nat Jones said, "Goober, since you're having such a time walking, you take charge of the critter. We'll go on ahead and tell the captain what you captured last night."

The three soldiers hurried off, leaving Len to take his time. When he reached camp, he discovered Jake Cooney and some of his friends lined up in ranks at each side of the road, hands raised to foreheads in mock-reverent salutes. They held a banner, which read:

*Welcome Back! General Goober and Dairy.*

Len's face was flaming as he went through camp and saw men grinning from every tent.

## 10          A SOLDIER'S DUTIES

Len's friends soon discovered that the cow was a good addition to the camp because of her milk. They scraped the area for fodder. Len was glad to substitute milk for the bitter black coffee he'd been drinking. The men made biscuits, corn pones, gravies, and puddings over the campfires, and gave him some.

Mr. Putnam presented Len with two pairs of new sox.

"No," said Len. "please don't. You keep them."

"Shucks, I've more than I need. Where's your worn ones? I'll darn them for you."

"No, sir. I'll darn them myself." Len didn't want the man to know he hadn't yet used his kit.

"Let me see you do it, then. You can do that now instead of having your fife lesson. You're going to need sox. There's a rumor the camp'll be breaking up."

"There *is!*"

"Seems the Rebs are getting too strong up the Rappahannock. I reckon we'll be moving on them."

"Good! I'm tired of sitting around here. It isn't like a war."

"Do up your sox right now, Son!" Mr. Putnam looked as if he meant business.

Len felt a little annoyed with his friend for ordering him to mend his sox. Yet the command made sense. Besides, Mr. Putnam had helped him a lot since they'd met. He'd made over Len's uniform, so it looked nice and fit him; he was teaching him to play the fife, had even given him his own fife; he was always watching over him the way Len remembered

his father's doing. Mr. Putnam would make a nice
father. Len wished he was his stepfather instead of
Mr. Thrace.

Mr. Putnam picked up the fife and trilled "The
Goober Galop." He kept his face turned away from
Len, as if he knew the boy would be embarrassed,
trying to darn when he didn't know how.

Len bit off some thread and thrust it through the
needle's eye. He put a stone inside his holey sock to
serve as a darning egg, as he'd seen Mr. Putnam do.
He pushed his needle in and out. It came unthreaded,
and he started over. The thread pulled completely
out of the sock, so he made a huge knot to hold it
there. Again he pushed his needle in and out, then
drew the weave up into a thick wad, tied another
knot, and tackled another hole.

Mr. Putnam played merry tunes, ignoring him.

When Len had finished, his sock was all gathered
up in bunches wherever there'd been a hole. Un-
accountably, it had become an inch too short. He'd
done the whole job wrong. He stuffed the sock into
his pocket where Mr. Putnam would not see it.

Then slowly he pulled it out. He might as well ad-

mit a mistake. Mr. Putnam could set him right. Anyone could see that those knots he'd tied and the
bunches of cloth he'd drawn up didn't look like Mr.
Putnam's neat darns and that Len's foot would get
rawer and more rubbed. There was no telling how
much marching was ahead, once camp broke up.

Swallowing his pride, Len humbly tapped Mr.
Putnam's elbow. "Better show me," he said.

As they worked together, Mr. Putnam said, "You
don't talk much about your folks. I believe you said
you had a stepfather."

"That's right."

"I imagine you thought a lot of your father."

"Yes, I did."

"And miss him."

"Of course."

"This other man, does he seem like a father to
you?"

Len glanced at his friend. That was a funny question. Mr. Putnam was getting rather personal. Len
wasn't sure he liked it. "He's all right, I guess."

"You guess, eh?" There was a moment's silence,
as if Mr. Putnam was searching for the right thing

to say. "It takes a little time for people to get used to each other, doesn't it? To know each other, I mean."

"Oh, I know *him* all right," Len answered, with bitterness showing in his voice.

"And don't like him," Mr. Putnam said softly.

"I didn't say that."

"No, but it's there, boy. Could you tell me why?"

"Well, would you like a man who picked on you all the time?"

Mr. Putnam whistled. "You're not the sort of boy one picks on. Is he a mean and vengeful man?"

Len turned the question over for several seconds. Was the Old Bean mean? Vengeful? He wanted to say yes immediately, yet something held him back.

"Did you do something bad?"

"It wasn't that," Len said sulkily.

"What was it then?"

Len scowled. "I didn't like him from the beginning. He said he wanted to be my father. I turned him down."

"That made it hard for him from the start," said Mr. Putnam. "Never mind the rest, Len. I understand a lot now. If only people could see inside each other. They make so many mistakes. I've made them, too." He got up, turned the fife up and down in his hands, then dropped it into Len's lap, and added, "I'm going off to see if the mail's come. It's been real queer that I ain't heard from Martha in three weeks."

He returned a short while later, his face more gaunt, a hunch to his shoulders. "No luck," he said, and shuffled past, his eyes mournful.

Len went to inquire for mail also, and was handed a package and a letter, which smelled of attar of roses. The letter was from Emily Jane, her first to him since adopting him as a pen companion. The package was from her, too. He opened it to find a dozen small white pebbles and an odd thing, crocheted of silk, from which dangled a tassel. What on earth was it? And why had she mailed him pebbles? The army camp was full of pebbles, all colors.

The explanation was in the note. "Dear Len, my Pen Companion, I have been told on good authority that soldiers on the march suffer considerably from thirst, and that a most efficacious solution to this

misery, when water is unavailable, is to hold a pebble
under the tongue. So I am sending you a small supply.

"Besides that, I enclose a nightcap. My father,
Judge Leonias Bradford, suffers from cold at night,
as his hair is sparse. In fact, he is bald, but combs
long hair from the side over the top for daytime wear.
At night he finds a cap most comfortable. So I have
made you one with my very own hands."

If such a package had come to anyone else, Len
would have burst his seams laughing. Instead, he
hastily pocketed the pebbles and thrust the cap out
of sight inside his shirt. He looked around, hoping
no one had seen what he had received, but the men
near him were reading letters or opening packages of
their own and did not glance up.

That girl! She had the craziest notions of anyone
he'd ever heard of. What would she do next? Pebbles! And a nightcap! When for two months now
he'd been sizzling with heat, besides having a thick
mop of brown hair to warm the top of his head.

Good guns and muskets!

# 11        "STRIKE TENTS!"

A few days later, as Len went back to his shelter tent after a long drill period, he encountered Mr. Putnam. At first Len didn't recognize him, he appeared so different. He was walking with a stumbling gait, and sort of wove his way along as if he couldn't see where he was going.

Len stopped. "Hello, sir."

The man didn't seem to hear him.

Len felt frightened. Something must be terribly wrong with him. He needed help. "Mr. Putnam!"

he said more loudly, but his friend just stumbled on, unheeding.

Len ran after him. "Hey! It's me! Len!"

A deep groan welled from Mr. Putnam's throat. He put his arm around Len and pressed the boy's head against his thin chest. "I've had a shock," he said finally. "My dear wife Martha has passed away."

Len understood how dreadful the man felt. Hadn't he gone through something similar when he lost his father? Mr. Putnam had been worried for weeks about his wife, because he'd not had letters from her, and now this was the explanation. She had doubtless been very ill for a long time.

"My children," the man said with effort. "Alone."

He started forward, still a little uncertain in his stride. Len walked along with him.

"I'll go to them. Captain issued me leave."

They reached Mr. Putnam's tent, and he began shuffling through his things, trying to pack.

"Leave them," Len urged. "I'll look after them for you."

"You're right. I won't need this stuff on my journey."

Mr. Putnam still seemed confused. He was very

pale. Len accompanied him to the quartermaster's tent, and found that a supply wagon would be departing within an hour. Mr. Putnam would be able to make connection with a stage to Washington, and then take the train to Germantown, Pennsylvania. By the next afternoon he would be with his children.

Getting under way seemed to relieve him. Mr. Putnam looked more like himself as he waved to Len from the wagon, although he was too sad to speak.

Len picked up his friend's army gear, leaving the half of canvas that was buttoned to the tentmate's half, so the other soldier would still have shelter. He moved Mr. Putnam's knapsack to his own tent.

In the middle of that same night Len's mate, Bill Harrison, shouted, "Wake up! Reveille!"

"Go on, you're dreaming," Len replied, still half asleep, but immediately he felt Bill push him.

An orderly appeared at the tent flap. "Strike tents! Form ranks."

The startled boys sprang into action. They knew what to do, because they had been given plenty of practice, but the real marching order, rousing them at night, made them fall all over themselves trying to collect their equipment and roll up their blankets and canvas pieces. Len found he had accumulated more stuff than the original army issue, including shirts, a writing case, books, and easy slippers, which he'd bought from the sutler.

He put a framed tintype of his mother into his inner jacket pocket and thrust the fife into another pocket, which Mr. Putnam had sewn into his jacket for that purpose. Into the crocheted nightcap Emily Jane had sent, he put his sewing kit and what was left of his lice salve. He had thrown away the pebbles long ago. His knife and several animals he'd been carving bulged out the back pocket of his trousers. That pocket probably would not pass inspection, but he couldn't bear to give up the carvings. They had taken him hours of work. Other items that wouldn't go into his knapsack he would have to leave behind, because he had to have room for rations.

Almost before the boys had buckled the last strap, the bugle blew. They ran to take up their positions for roll call.

Three-days' rations were issued to all the men, not to just a unit or two. It looked as if the whole camp was leaving, being broken up for good.

Len glanced around the stretch of open ground,

now completely bare except for the tent poles, many of which had been left standing. Lumps of rubbish lay on the campsite. Len and Bill weren't the only ones who'd accumulated more than they could carry. Otherwise, everything was gone, except the beaten paths the men's feet had made between the tents.

Suddenly Len gulped. He'd forgotten Mr. Putnam's knapsack. It lay with the things he'd thrown away. He'd have to get it. He'd promised to look after it. Mr. Putnam would be back with the company eventually, and he'd need everything in his knapsack, and his blanket, too.

Len dashed up to his officer, Major Jeffers, for permission to go to the tent site.

"Young man! I thought we'd taught you army routine. Get along with you, but make it back on the double quick!"

"Yes, sir!"

He dragged the knapsack up onto his shoulders on top of his own. The straps gnawed into his flesh. He knew he looked a fright under the load. How was he ever going to march in the ranks staggering under two knapsacks? He might have to walk miles!

To his dismay, he found that the drum corps was to lead. The color bearer was at the head, then the

band. They were to go out of camp in style. Maybe
the high officers were to watch them. He would be
thrown out of the corps if he went along looking like
a camel.

"Goober!" A hand reached out from the line and
grabbed him. "Haven't you got any sense?"

It was Jake Cooney. The soldier was evidently so
amazed by Len's appearance he couldn't make a
joke as usual.

"It's Mr. Putnam's!" Len cried. "You know what's
happened. I'll ditch my own pack before I will his!"

"Good boy, Goob!" Jake slapped Len's back so
roughly he nearly knocked him down. "But you don't
need to carry the fellow's stuff. They'll take it on the
supply wagon. Tell them about it."

There was just time to make the arrangement and
get back into position, when the orders sounded.
The company marched away under the rising sun,
with Len earnestly trilling on his fife.

Out of the corner of his eye he saw the Confederate cow, lonesomely wandering among the tent
poles. The sight made him feel sad. She had been
everybody's pet, and his especially. Once more she
was being abandoned.

# 12                ON THE MARCH

Len never forgot the two weeks that followed. Although the company set off buoyantly on a fine brick road through flat, open country, it soon reached a road with a surface of red clay, which had baked dry and then crumbled. Now the dust rose around the men in clouds, coating their clothes, getting into their nostrils, choking them, and growing so thick they could barely see each other. The sun burned through the dust, until their faces were striped with rivulets of sweat. Swarms of biting flies pestered them.

The band no longer had to play. Len put his fife away, and hoped it wasn't too clogged to operate.

After an interval the dust cloud attracted enemy fire from a grove of trees. The company was peppered with flying bullets, but marched on doggedly, although several men were struck. The Reb fire ceased as abruptly as it had started, and Len wondered if the enemy had been put to rout by an unseen branch of the Union Army.

The drum corps now marched behind the army wagons, whose drivers swore mightily at the stubborn mules they had to urge along. In front of each wagon was a toolbox; in back, a feed trough. A wooden bucket for water hung from one rear axle; from the other, an iron bucket for grease.

Len's feet were soon raw again, for calluses had not yet formed on them. Since many of the men were breaking ranks to kick off their shoes and wade through the dust barefoot, he stopped, too. His knapsack seemed to grow heavier with every step. H struggled forward and slipped it into the feed trough.

"No, you don't!" someone yelled from the wagon. "Get that outa there!"

He had to return the sack to his back, but first he

examined it, wondering if there was anything he could discard. His hardtack ration was all he felt like dumping, but he didn't dare. This supply seemed to be free of weevils, so he had no excuse for throwing it out and asking for a replacement. In fact, there would be no replacements, for the food-supply wagons had not accompanied them, but were on the way to Alexandria, Virginia, to be replenished.

Some of the band corps were carrying heavier loads than he. They, too, had accumulated possessions while in camp. Bill had a rope, a slat hammock, a dozen candles, a prayer book, a small mirror, and two extra shirts. As the heat bore down and everyone's fatigue increased, Len saw men discarding things. Bill tossed away the rope and his sword—the toad-sticker—and, later, the candles and hammock. Finally all Bill's extras were gone, even his prayer book.

Len was so thirsty he couldn't keep away from his canteen. Soon it was empty, and he had to stagger along through the dust with a parched mouth.

Suddenly a cheer burst out from the ranks. A short halt had been ordered. It seemed like heaven to the men, especially when they discovered themselves to be within a few rods of a pond. The whole company was soon splashing in swampy water that smelled horribly of decaying vegetation. But it was cool and refreshing, the best water they'd ever encountered, they thought.

Len stripped, and soused himself. Nothing had ever felt so good. He cupped his hand for a drink. The water was dirty and muddy, full of green algae, but he didn't care, he'd drink anyway.

A fist slapped his hand away from his mouth. "You little fool! You'll get sick as a dog!" He saw Jake Cooney glaring at him. "No sense whatever, that's you. No wonder Putnam asked me one day to keep an eye on you."

Indignantly Len smacked his hands against the water, aiming a sheet of it into Jake's face. "He didn't!" he cried furiously. "Mr. Putnam's left on furlough. Anyway, I can look after myself, you snoop!"

Jake wiped his face with the back of his hand. "He asked me to, Goober, and for good reason, I'd say. You should know better than to drink swamp water."

When the march started again, the air was clear,

and the men felt better. The ranks had broken, the soldiers walking by two's or four's or straggling in single lines. They crossed fields and went through woods.

Len was annoyed to discover Jake walking behind him. He forged ahead to get away from him. He scowled, thinking over what Jake had said, that Mr. Putnam had told him to keep an eye on him. His fellow soldiers acted sometimes as if they thought him weak in the head. Look how Mr. Black and Mr. Hickman had avoided talking about the skirmish, doubtless because of the blood. Nat Jones had come up to see how he was faring while on picket duty, as if he was too green to serve as a sentinel. Mr. Putnam used up his free time teaching Len fifing and doing him favors. Now Jake, instead of playing jokes, was starting to give him advice.

He turned around and confronted him. "From now on, mind your own business!" he cried.

"Why, Goober! That's no way to talk to a big feller like me. Don't you know I could lick you with one fingernail?"

"I don't need a supervisor, so let me alone!"

"You're a smart little cock, ain't you?" Jake pulled his mouth down. "All right, Goob, it's your neck you're sticking out. Good luck!"

Jake joined some of his friends, and Len trudged on, wishing he'd never spoken. After a while he glanced around, and was chilled by the look of complete indifference Jake showed as their eyes met. Len felt his heart sink. That was what he'd asked for—indifference—and now he didn't like it.

At that moment Jake made a clown face, crossing his eyes and pulling his mouth to one side. He began to bawl the goober song, which he'd sung the first days they were in camp together. " 'What do you think he sees? The Geor-gi-a militia eating goober peas!' "

Len dropped back to walk beside him. "Dumbbell," he said affectionately.

"Cuckoo!" answered Jake.

Mile after mile, the company plodded on. Len felt so tired he could hardly lift his feet. Would they never be allowed to stop? They had to eat as they walked, nibbling at their rations. Only in the late afternoon was a second halt called, and then just long enough for them to refill their canteens at a brook.

They returned to a road. Now the walking was good, for the dust had been laid by a shower. Finally, two hours after sunset, they were told to make camp. Soldiers lit a campfire and began boiling coffee. Len cut a long stick, held his strips of pork over the flames, let the grease drip down on his hardtack to soften it, and lapped the whole thing up with smacking lips. He was too hungry to remember his usual distaste for army food.

He didn't want to bother with a tent, so went off by himself to sleep. Bill would probably do the same. Len had learned it was wise to build up the ground under him to keep himself dry. But since this soil was already dry, he didn't disturb it, just threw himself in a bare spot, free of ants, and was instantly asleep.

Rain awakened him. He hadn't put up his canvas or protected himself in any way. He lay in a puddle, and was soaked through. He'd slept in rain at the base camp, but the summer rains had been warm. Now

it was late September. This rain felt cold. He got up
wearily and tried to squeeze water from his soggy
uniform.

Len wasn't the only one who hadn't pitched a tent
that night. Soldiers were huddled about the campfire.
He went over to warm up. The fire was so feeble it
threw no heat. In fact, the men could hardly keep the
flame alive, with nothing but wet sticks to use and
with the rain sifting down in a fine spray. The hot
coffee was a help. Len drank, then squatted on a
stone, wrapped his arms around his legs, put his
head down on his knee, and slept again.

The first day's march was only a sampling of the
discomforts Len was to encounter. After marching in
rain all the next day, he pitched tent with Bill, only
to have the tent blow down. The canvas lay across
them, letting the water through. He and Bill crawled
into another tent with two companions. They were
barely settled when the wind changed, and drove the
rain straight in on them. The four soldiers crowded
together, trying to get warm, trying to sleep. A few
minutes after they'd dropped off, the bugle sounded.

It was about three A.M., and dark. At first Len and
Bill couldn't locate their canvas strips. They had

blown away and been confiscated by a pair of soldiers, who had strung them up as a windbreak, and were found crouched behind them, wrapped in blankets.

Len heard pickets firing. "We're near the lines," he heard someone say.

The company was ordered to get into battle formation. The officers moved about in the lantern light, conferring. There was an uneasiness in their actions that made the men feel an attack was expected.

Len saw a messenger from the pickets rush into camp. News spread among the men that a corporal and three privates had been lost. They'd been decoyed outside the lines and captured.

The company moved backward several miles on its route, pushing through heavy rain and listening to the rattle of distant musketry and the roar of artillery. Things had changed fast since they'd left the base camp. They were brought to a halt. They turned in upon the ground, sleeping as best they could out in the open. The men felt it was too near dawn and reveille to bother setting up shelters.

Len slept heavily until the sound of people stirring around him woke him up. He found that a large force of cavalry had arrived, and was making camp. All his

cold and dampness were forgotten. He sprang up and
went excitedly from one tethered horse to another,
stroking the beasts and admiring them.

"What you doing, soldier?" one of the cavalrymen
called out. "Want to get kicked to kingdom come?"

Len sidled off in disappointment. He was doing no
harm. Couldn't he even look at a horse?

"They've got too many kids in the army," he heard
the man say to someone else. "Look at that one."

Len slunk off, feeling as bad as if he had been
kicked.

# 13        THROUGH VIRGINIA

Back and forth the company went, making long, wearisome marches, yet seeming to remain in the same area. Some days the firing was very close. Len expected that at any moment they'd come to grips with the enemy, only to learn they were retreating.

"What's the matter?" he asked one of his comrades.

"The Rebs are too strong for us. We've been licked wherever we've fought, almost."

"We haven't even seen them!"

"Not us in this company. We're running a flanking movement and trying to keep routes blocked, so the Rebs can't run through reinforcements and supplies."

Len felt better after that about the marches, which had seemed to go futilely here and there as if the officers couldn't make up their minds where to send the army. The men were dispirited, though, for they had learned that a huge Union contingent had fought along the Rappahannock and been defeated, with the loss of hundreds of men, dead or wounded or captured. Part of Len's company departed. When none of the men returned after several days, faces grew grave. That night the pickets were driven in, and the camp was in an upheaval, as the men hurried to erect breastworks of trees and fence rails, which they raked up wherever they could.

Across the fields enemy infantry opened fire. Shells began to whiz overhead. An enemy battery had been sneaked close in on them and cleverly hidden. Now it popped shells at short range. The startled soldiers ran to the nearest trees for cover, as the officers ordered retreat.

Len didn't feel very brave. He ran for dear life; yet he felt sheepish. Shouldn't they have taken a stand?

This was his company's first encounter with the enemy, and all they'd done was to take to their heels. They hadn't fired a shot in return. It was disgraceful. The North would never win if that was the way the army fought.

Then he learned that their action had been a feint. Without his being aware of it, part of the company had turned in behind the Confederates and joined Union reinforcements. They had forced the Rebs back. The Yanks had captured the enemy battery of three guns.

This victorious skirmish cheered the company a little, but there was much pessimistic talk around the campfires. Many of the men were sick of war, and longed to go peacefully back to their wives and children.

Len sat listening. He thought of his mother. How he'd like to see her! He was glad she was far up North in a safe place. The soldiers had passed farmsteads, denuded by both armies, the fruit taken from the trees, the vegetables carried off. Len had seen the women who had stayed on the farms, working with hoes, trying to salvage onions, corn, potatoes, carrots, and yams overlooked by the armies. The women

looked gaunt from overwork, anxiety, and hunger.
They stared at the Yanks with dread showing in their
eyes, afraid that the men would rob them of the little
food that remained.

Back in Massachusetts, Len's mother was safe from
such misery, and he was glad. But he felt uncomfortable over the wreck being made of the beautiful
Virginia countryside. He saw blackened frames of
houses, burned by the army; stumps and shattered
trees; torn-up bridges; and roads, blasted with dynamite to keep supply wagons from getting through.
Railway warehouses, which had held quantities of
grain, flour, sugar, and other stores, had been destroyed. The railroad stations had also been burned,
along with the surrounding track. For miles in places
the track was a welter of twisted rail, with wrecked
locomotives and stripped trains of cars marooned
between the blasted areas.

Len knew that the secessionists were bound to
suffer more from this destruction than the Northern
armies, for here lay their homes and their source of
supplies. The Southern railways were badly laid out
for transportation, and there were too few of them. In
some areas there were no railroad lines at all, and even

the Union men had trouble forcing through their ammunition and food.

Len listened one day as an old gentleman talked to the colonel. Len's company was camping in the man's oat field. The house was roofless, and had been partially burned.

"Sir," he said to the colonel, "I've only one thing left—an old, old horse. Your men won't want to eat him. They've already taken my two-year-old heifer and butchered her, and are carrying her down the road on the points of their bayonets. I'm told you are destroying thirty-thousand bushels of oats today. Please, will you let me have some for my horse?"

Len waited tensely, not daring to look at the colonel, for fear the pleading he knew must be in his own eyes would harden the officer's heart. Army commanders were not allowed to be compassionate to enemy people. The old man was a Southerner, possibly in sympathy with the secessionists. However, he was not a soldier, but a victim of the war. Len knew how *he* would answer. Would the colonel feel the same?

The officer spoke brusquely, looking stiff and uncompromising as he stared over the old man's head.

"Take what you can before we leave," he snapped.

That would not mean many bushels, but Len felt his heart lift. He was sure the man would be able to carry off enough oats to keep his horse from starving that winter.

Mail came. Len's mother inquired if he was happy. What was he doing? Was he in danger? He could read worry between every line.

Mr. Thrace enclosed a note. "I'd be glad if you were home." And Edie sent a fruitcake, somewhat crushed in the shipment, but oozing goodness from every crumb.

His brother Will wrote that he wished Len was safe at home getting his education. "When it was pleasant and comfortable for you, why did you stick your neck into this noose? You did not need to enlist. I was stupefied when I heard you ran off and enlisted. I can't figure out how you got in at your age. The folks at home don't seem to know, either, and speak vaguely of some 'friend' to whom you appealed. Friend! As far as I'm concerned, that was no friend. I'd like to speak my mind to him."

Will then wrote of his duties as hospital steward,

and described how sad it made him to go out on the battlefield hunting for wounded and finding so many men dead. "I am thankful for my small knowledge of medicine. It has helped me save more than one life. I am now more determind than ever to become a doctor."

Emily Jane also wrote to her pen companion. "I'll be nearer you, dear boy, for my father, Judge Leonias Bradford, has decided to move our goods and chattels to Washington for the duration of the conflict. He is lonely without me, and also wishes me to serve as hostess, since he must entertain some of the leaders of our government fairly frequently. Mrs. Stebbins will continue to serve as our housekeeper."

She sent him a new comb and brush, which he received thankfully. The teeth and bristles were nearly gone from his old ones, due to the rigorous way he attacked his hair every day, trying to get rid of the eternal nits.

Len thought often of Mr. Putnam, wishing he had news of him. He felt sorry for him, and understood now why his friend had fretted and been uneasy, although it had bored him at first, because it had contrasted with his own gay feeling about the war. Now he worried about Mr. Putnam's knapsack. The wagon to which he'd consigned it had not yet reappeared. Len checked each time a supply outfit arrived. Mr. Putnam would be hard put if he lost all his equipment.

Then one day Mr. Putnam came back. As he stepped down off the wagon, he looked solemnly at the trousers and shirts flapping in the trees from the men's laundering. Len stared, recognizing his friend's knapsack with its familiar hand-stitched initials. Mr. Putnam clasped his hand warmly, and smiled a little when he saw Len looking in puzzlement at the knapsack.

"It was stored for me in Washington. I wrote in about it after my wits cleared a little. I knew you couldn't handle it, once you left base camp. . . . I've had quite a time," he went on. "It fair breaks my heart to think what I've done with the children, now my wife's gone. We had no relatives to help. Our neighbors are burdened with their own responsibilities. There was nothing for it but to put my two poor youngsters into an orphanage till the war's over and I can go home."

Len gasped. An orphanage! Edie had been raised

in one, and he'd heard her tell how she'd suffered from both hunger and cruelty. She'd longed for friendship and affection from the directors and teachers, only to have them be cold and indifferent. All they'd seemed interested in, Edie had said, was to make harsh rules, and then whip any child who broke them. Mr. Putnam's children were going to be mighty lonely.

"They both cried considerably, even the boy, and he doesn't like to show his feelings. They didn't want to see me leave. It fair broke my heart." Mr. Putnam sighed. "I can go on furlough to see them, of course, only it won't be often. They're still going to be very unhappy."

"I'm glad you're back," Len said shyly, and meant it. He had missed Mr. Putnam more than he'd realized. He changed the subject, feeling a little embarrassed by his surge of emotion. "They've started using Sibley tents—platoon tents, they call them— because the weather's getting bad. I don't like them. You have to lie among about twelve fellows with your hooves toward the center, and you either get kicked, or else one fellow thinks he's a clown and hops around keeping everyone awake, playing funny.

Or if anyone is called out for duty, it's sure to be the man farthest from the opening, and he climbs over everyone and steps on them. The tents smell, too, because none of us gets a chance to bathe, and some fellows close them up and then smoke all night. Bill's gone into one, though—he gave me his canvas. I like being by myself. I sleep better. . . . Your old tentmate is in a Sibley, too."

Len paused, fumbled with his belt a minute, and added, "Would you like to come in with me, sir?"

A wide, pleased smile appeared on Mr. Putnam's face, the first happy look Len had seen on him for a long time. "Well now, that's right kind of you. But are you sure you want it that way? I take up a lot of room, even when I let my feet hang outside."

"Come on."

"Maybe it'll work out," Mr. Putnam said. "Maybe we can organize our sacks, so you don't carry so much weight. I'll take the brunt. We'll shift as much to my back as regulations allow. How's that?"

"I get along all right, as is," Len said.

"You look a little poorly, boy, from when I last saw you."

"I'm fine."

"I brought us each a rubber blanket—weighs light. With them tucked around us, we're going to lie free of an awful lot of dampness."

"Hey! That's the best yet!"

The daily marches continued, with reveille at four or five in the morning. Often only small fires were permitted for cooking, so the men ate their food raw. Sometimes the day was burning hot and Len's thirst unbearable. Once he was so desperate for water he sluiced it up from the muddy pools that formed in the men's footprints. He wet his lips, not daring to swallow such a drink. But the water the men used for their coffee was just as muddy.

In the autumn the streams were brown and sluggish between rains. Len was sent out occasionally on picket duty with a comrade. They lay low in the brush while Minié balls whizzed over them. They could sometimes see their own men creeping down hillsides, moving relentlessly toward danger. They had to remain quiet and keep the enemy under watch until he gave away his plans. Then the two pickets would sneak back with the information.

Sometimes, when the company went into battle

formation, Len was called out by Captain Hockness to serve as orderly. He had to remain in camp, and see Bill march by, beating his drum, and see Mr. Putnam, Jake Cooney, Nat Jones, all the men he knew, go past with muskets over their shoulders. When the brigade returned a day or so later, he was still on duty and unable to run out and find his friends, but he listened as best he could to roll call.

As the weeks passed, roll call became the most disheartening moment of the day. The number of men who did not answer grew larger and larger, because they had been left on the battlefield wounded or dead, or perhaps had been captured by the enemy. At first no one knew the exact cause of their absence. Then the hospital list came through, followed by prison lists and death lists. All of it was grim.

Len could hardly bear to write a letter home or to Will. What could he say that would not reveal the weight he felt of the suffering around him? The men were short of sleep, hungry, and low in spirits, because there were too many retreats and defeats, and the losses were too heavy for the gains they made over the Rebs. They did not look like a glorious army now in their worn, mud-streaked clothes, in which they even had to sleep. Their hair was long and unkempt, their beards matted, their faces dirty, their eyes red from strain. Many had minor wounds, which they tended themselves, because the hospital corps was far too busy with the desperately wounded even to look at them. Many men were sick with malaria, dysentery, grippe, and fevers, but stayed in camp only when too weak to walk or carry a gun.

How could he write? What could he say?

Finally he began describing Mr. Putnam, telling his family how companionable the man had turned out to be. He told them of the hundreds of gay tunes Mr. Putnam knew and played for Len and the men on the fife they now shared. He organized things so cleverly that their sleeping quarters were the most comfortable Len had yet experienced. He collected branches, dry leaves, and hay to make a mattress, and carried a set of pegs to pin down the canvas at night. He scratched out ditches to drain away the rains and keep the blankets dry under the rubber ones he'd brought. He knew games and tricks, which he taught to the soldiers, but which he taught to Len first. He did all this, although frequently he was staggering with fatigue.

It wasn't long before Len noticed that the main campfire was built before their tent, and that the first cup of coffee went to Mr. Putnam, who promptly poured half of it into Len's cup. The men presented him with berries or fruits they'd jayhawked from the countryside. Altogether Mr. Putnam was the most popular man in camp.

"You sure have friends," Len remarked.

"I like people," Mr. Putnam answered.

"You put yourself out a lot."

"Well, I like having friends. I figger that to have friends, one should be a good friend. A lot of these men are plagued by what they're going through here, to say nothing of having troubles at home. I ought to know. So when I came back, I thought I'd try to cheer things up if I could. The funny thing about it is, it sort of eases me. Works two ways, I guess, and I don't feel so bad about Martha." His sad eyes stared into Len's. "Not that I'll ever quite forget. Also, I'm still fretted over my kids. Hope they don't think I'm a bad daddy, especially the boy."

"Why him?"

"Because he's old enough to get notions. He hates

that orphanage. I don't want him to feel about me the way you do about your stepfather."

Len looked hard at the ground. Mr. Putnam was trying to tell him something—point out something. Len could tell from the solemn way the man watched him.

"Dick must see you couldn't help but put him there," Len said finally.

"But if he gets his back up and takes a notion I should have done something else, I'm going to be in a bad box."

Again Len sensed a message for him, but he shrugged it off. "Show me that trick again, the one where the coin turns up in your ear."

"You're going to have to do it yourself from now on. Once more I'll show you, then you're on your own."

## 14         THE ADVANCE

Len was chosen so often to serve as orderly that he began to suspect the officers of intentionally trying to keep him out of danger. Some of the time he had so little to do that he whittled a dozen animals out of sheer boredom.

"I want to go with the band," he told Mr. Putnam. "Bill says I'm missing the fun, relaying signals and then watching the army turn and follow, knowing just where to charge. That's useful. What good am I, carrying messages from one post to another, making

coffee for the officers? Never see a thing happen. Just
see the cannon smoke rising or hear the guns. What
good is that?"

"It takes all of us," Mr. Putnam said. "And your
kind of job counts."

"The officers tell me about their kids. What makes
me boil is they say their sons are about my age; then
they look at me."

"Why shouldn't they look at you?"

"Well, they—" Len was about to add, "They
think I should be home, too," but caught himself. It
wasn't true. He was imagining things. No officer
would think a soldier under him should be home.
The army needed men too badly. He was a good
soldier, and had proved it every day by carrying out
orders, marching, or playing his fife. What if the
officers did guess he was younger than his papers
showed—he was still a badly needed soldier. Oh,
surely he was! He could be still more useful if they'd
let him onto a battlefield.

Before many days there were signs that a great
charge against the enemy was to start. Cavalry units
rode in and made camp. Wagons moved along rutted
roads, dragging artillery and food supplies.

"Len," Mr. Putnam said, as they lay in their shelter tent the night before their departure, "you play 'The Goober Galop' as well as I do. I like hearing you."

"It's my favorite tune."

"Keep playing it." Mr. Putnam raised up on his elbow. "I wouldn't mind if you never forgot it the rest of your life."

Next morning, when the bugles sounded through the darkness, the two friends hurried to strike tent. Len took time, however, to give Mr. Putnam a package. "It's for your kids."

Mr. Putnam immediately lighted a candle and opened the package. "I swan! When did you make these?" He examined the small doll and the two wooden ships Len had presented to him. "I never noticed you working on them."

"The boats are the *Merrimac* and the *Monitor*. I thought Dick would like them."

"Certain sure. And Lucy's going to love the wee doll. Goober boy, that's right nice of you."

"I never made a doll before. I think the head's too big."

"It's fine. These things will make my poor youngsters feel better. It bothers me night and day that they're not happy anymore." He blew out the candle, rewrapped the package, and put it into a wallet in his jacket pocket where, like most of the soldiers, he kept military and identification papers and his most important small possessions.

A half hour later they were on their way, Len, a small figure in a vast array of tall armed men of several companies that had joined together this day. He saw skirmishers far ahead, a thin line of men going through the trees, with guns at the ready for picket attacks. Jake Cooney was among them.

Almost at once a rifle shot was heard, then scattered shots, then a rattling volley like sudden rain on a metal roof. Enemy pickets and a hidden battery were on the alert and shooting at the skirmishers.

Len wondered what effect the shooting would have on the advance, and half expected a counterorder and the usual retreat. Instead, the officers repeated their earlier instructions. On no account was any soldier to stop on the battlefield to aid, give succor, assist, or help a wounded fellow soldier in any way, even though the wounded man might plead for all he was worth, or even though he might be a relative, such as a brother, son, or father. Under no circumstances, the officer said again. As for looting the dead—

Len shuddered. There'd been plenty of that. He'd heard men talk. He couldn't imagine how anyone could steal the pitiful little treasures of a man who had given his life for his country. Of what value were the rings, coins, and small souvenirs of a dead man to a thief, who must fight a bad conscience forever after?

As for helping the wounded—someone suffering, needing water, needing a kind hand to ease his pain—how was Len to obey an order not to stop? He bit his lips hard. What was he to do? Then he thought of his brother Will, who was a steward in the hospital corps. This corps sought out the wounded, often during battle, at great risk of life. Sometimes soldiers had to lie in agony for hours before help came. Many died before they could be rescued. During battle that was what happened. War brought every known misery.

Suddenly Len was unable to see his usual vision of flying flags and men on parade, which he always thought of as he marched off. He saw only the grim, unhappy faces of men primed for battle, primed to kill other men, even their brothers, if they were enemies to the Northern cause.

And what was he to do if a wounded man called to him for help? There was nothing for it but to obey orders and to hope and pray that brave men like Will were following close behind with the stretchers and wagons that would carry the wounded away.

From his place in the drum corps Len glanced behind him. He was glad Mr. Putnam was tall. He was easy to spot in the ranks. He was standing with his gun over his shoulder. The haunted look on his face made Len wonder if he, too, was disturbed by the order. Yet, unlike Len, he had been in skirmishes several times already. He was probably thinking of something else. Maybe of his children.

All was quiet for a while. The sound of artillery was distant, and they seemed to be circling it, tramping over the usual impossible roads, which were either hard and rutted, or a welter of mud, sometimes half-way up their shins.

When the road was good, the drum corps was ordered to play and the men to keep step. It was thus that Len's company started over a bridge on the Rapidan River. As they advanced, the bridge began to sway. The men heard ominous creakings and pop-pings, and glanced at each other in consternation.

Had the bridge been mined by the enemy? Would it collapse and drop them all into the river?

"It's the cursed music!" a colonel roared. He ordered the drum corps to be silent and the men to walk out of step. The swaying stopped immediately.

The army went through a Virginia town, with orders to march smartly as if to impress the inhabitants, for this was an enemy town. The Yanks saw shattered buildings, broken chimneys, windows boarded up, brick walls scarred from direct hits, piles of ashes and half-burned boards, where the army had set fire to wooden sidewalks and fences.

The town was being spared further shelling due to the presence of Southern wounded, hundreds of whom had been stuffed into two churches serving as hospitals, but without nurses or doctors. There were none available in the stricken village. The women did what they could without medicine and without enough food for the sufferers.

On the streets the soldiers saw only women and children, who glared at them with fear and hate in their eyes. Any men or boys who were still about were doubtless in hiding to avoid being taken prisoner. However, as the army toiled gravely through town, even the women and children disappeared. Len felt their hidden eyes resentfully watching the passing troops from shuttered windows.

Reports went through the ranks that there had been a Union victory that morning near the town. Len felt little elation, although the news seemed to cheer the men. They had undergone many defeats in the region up to now. They hoped that this victory would bring a turn of the tide.

Len's company went over the Rapidan again, this time on a pontoon bridge, replacing one that had been dynamited. At another crossing they passed through lines of troops, holding a recently captured ferry. Then they went into a wood, filled with sheep taken from the enemy. The men licked their lips. "Maybe we'll get some of that mutton in our rations," a drummer at Len's side said hopefully. But the men marched on and on, far from any prospect of such a treat.

As usual, Len's feet complained long before the march ended. He had kept his sox darned and spare pairs on hand, but now there were holes in his shoes, which let in gravel and sand. The weather had grown much colder, for it was October, and he could not walk barefoot. He hobbled and limped along, his feet bleeding and hurting. Whenever there was a halt, he tried to cover the holes in his shoes by tying pieces of bark in place, and he made pads of grass to soften the inside, where the leather rubbed his toes. Unfortunately the repairs soon worked loose. At fords he waded across barefoot, glad for the feel of water, even though it stung.

They reached a region where all the bridges were gone, and yet, due to the winding of the river, they had to cross and recross it. Len suddenly found Mr. Putnam beside him. "Watch out for potholes," his friend cautioned. "If you hit one, you'll go in up to your ears."

Despite the gun he must keep dry, Mr. Putnam managed to hang onto Len's shoulder when they were in water nearly up to Len's neck and the current was too strong for him. A number of men slipped and were carried downstream, but managed to struggle ashore. At the next crossing a cavalry-man hauled a rope from one side to the other, and the soldiers clung to it to keep their balance. At a still worse ford a company of cavalry made a wall across the stream with their horses. After that a small number of mounted men were present at all fords to rescue soldiers who lost their footing.

The men were so wet at the end of the first day's march that they streamed water like pressed sponges as they made camp and hastily built fires for drying out their clothes. They shook with cold. Even the hot coffee they drank almost at the boiling point failed to warm them up.

Len carried his mother's picture and his papers inside a rubber pouch he had made. He had wrapped his blanket around this. The blanket was in turn enclosed in the rubber blanket Mr. Putnam had given him and, although it had been doused more than once, it was dry.

With the blanket wrapped around him, he gathered wood to refuel the fire, and joined the men holding their clothes on sticks over it. Steam rose like a fog. The dripping all but stifled the flames. Len despaired of ever getting his clothes dry. He wrung out a wool vest he had bought from the sutler, then edged a hot stone out from the bed of the fire, wrapped it in leaves to keep it from burning the cloth, and laid the vest around the stone. To his delight, it dried. He clapped it around his shivering body.

"Goober!" Jake Cooney yelled at him. "Give me that stone!" But by then it was too cold to be of use.

The men passed an almost sleepless night in only half-dried uniforms under damp blankets. Some crouched by the fires all night, frying on one side, freezing on the other. In the morning they found the ground white with frost and their clothes sleeted with ice. Many of the men were concerned about their possessions, the little private things from home each one carried and cherished. Too much wetting was destroying them.

The first ford that morning aroused deep groans. At the river halt Len saw Jake Cooney and Mr. Putnam conferring. The two usually kept track of each other when their duties made it possible. He'd discovered that between them they usually kept track of him, too, as he did of them.

"Goob," Jake cried, "this ford's too deep for you. We're going to set you on a couple of poles and tote you over."

"Shucks, I can make it," Len said. "I'll hang on to the rope or a horse's tail or something."

"No, you won't. You're riding, and in return you can carry all our stuff up over your head and keep it dry. We're going to collect enough from the men to fill a knapsack for you to hold. That way you'll be more useful than drowning on us."

The method worked so well that other short soldiers were carried over, too.

From his perch Len spotted a shoe, snagged on a tree branch in midstream, and grabbed it. On shore he eagerly tried it on. The shoe was an inch too long, but was whole and dry. By wearing two pairs of sox and putting padding in the toe, he was able to make one poor sore foot comfortable.

After three days of marching Len and Mr. Putnam woke up one morning to hear the sound of shelling quite close. They began dressing and getting packed for the day. Reveille had not yet roused the encampment, so they were able to linger over their chores.

Mr. Putnam kept glancing at Len. Finally he straightened his thin shoulders and said resolutely, "We haven't much time nowadays to talk things over. Maybe in all the confusion we'll be in from now on, we won't be able to camp together anymore, so I want to tell you something—something you don't know about me, Goober. Now listen. I think a great deal of Dick. I *love* the boy, I might say."

Why shouldn't he? Len thought. He's Dick's father. It's automatic. Why mention it?

"I love him. I did so from the first. I wanted a son like him, and was glad to get him. He's a fine boy, Goober; yet I had a problem with him. Guess what it was."

"I don't know." Len shrugged. He was not especially interested.

"It was a serious problem, Len. Fact is, Dick is a stepson. Not my own boy."

Len's breath caught in surprise. Here was something he'd never suspected. He had not given much thought to Mr. Putnam's children, except for feeling sorry for them when they lost their mother and were sent to live in an orphanage. Now he realized that Mr. Putnam had purposely not told him about his relationship to Dick. Why?

Len glanced up into the eyes studying him so gravely. He wriggled uncomfortably, sensing that his friend had something more of significance to say to him.

"You claim you don't like your stepfather," Mr. Putnam said. "That's the way Dick felt at first. He got over it, but he had me worried for a while."

"Any kid would like you, once he knew you."

"Dick didn't at first. He was real ornery, and it broke my heart, his sulking and sassing and resenting me, when he was really such a fine laddie—like you. Did you know that you're a pretty fine young un?"

"That's slush," Len said, turning red to the ears, but inwardly feeling pleased.

"I think your Mr. Thrace must feel bad. Have you ever thought of that?"

"Mr. Thrace? What does he care?"

"That's just it. Just what does he care? As near as I can make out, you've never given it a thought. You've seen only your side. How about it, Len? Have you ever tried to put yourself in Mr. Thrace's place as regards you as a stepson and him as a stepfather?"

"Nope."

"Hm!" Mr. Putnam rubbed his chin, as if reflecting what to add next. "I guess I won't say more. Maybe you're not ready for the idea yet, but I want to tell you that the little happiness I have left now, since my wife's death, is knowing that Dick, my stepson, is as fond of me as little Lucy, who is my own and his mother's child and his half sister. He remembers his father, but he feels I can substitute.

As I say, this cheers me up. I think it gives him something, too, to lean on—to have a substitute for his
father."

"But you're a swell person!" Len cried.

"And Mr. Thrace is a brute, just an old, mean,
cruel, heartless skunk, is he not?"

"No!" Len exclaimed. He clamped his mouth
shut, grabbed up his knapsack, and fled. He couldn't
stand any more of this talk. It made him feel queer—
all mixed up and filled with doubts.

Mr. Putnam was nice, and Mr. Thrace was not.
He liked Mr. Putnam, and he didn't like Mr. Thrace.
The only thing he could see clearly at this minute
was that although Mr. Thrace had made him furious
from the first by being a bully, he had been that way
mostly when Len had sassed him or cut school. Len
had to admit that in all honesty. But that was *all!*

He stamped off to the campfire, wishing he could
forget Mr. Thrace. To think that his best friend in
camp had dragged in the Old Bean and tried to make
Len feel there was any similarity in the two stepfather
situations. There just wasn't, Len told himself crossly.

## 15    TIRED, HUNGRY, AND COLD

The troops set off on the day's march with no sus-
picion that they would tramp for several days before
food rations were given out again. They carelessly
devoured everything, and even threw away biscuits
and tins to lighten their loads. They were negligent
about water, for they were less thirsty in the cooler
weather, and did not bother to fill their canteens,
thinking they could do so at any time.

Len threw away his hardtack. He was having wee-
vil trouble again. "I won't eat worms!" he cried, feel-

ing sick at his stomach at the very sight of the creatures.

His hunger increased with every step. There wasn't
a crumb of anything in his sack. The tinned meat, the
salt pork, the beans, all gone. He dragged along, so
weak and tired he could hardly lift his feet.

They no longer marched in ranks. The men plodded along like wooden robots, their faces set, not
daring to think of their hunger. They were so weary
they were barely aware of anything but the bumpy,
broken road. Sometimes someone dropped down
onto a stone, groaning, and rested a minute, but felt
ashamed to linger when all his fellow soldiers resolutely staggered past. Len stole rests, too.

Night came, and still they marched. Morning
came, and they were allowed to stop only once, to
fill their canteens. On they went. The dawn light
came palely through mists shrouding the woods.

Len was cold. At home they'd all be snug in their
beds at this hour. The house would be warm. In the
kitchen cupboard there'd be a roast, maybe a bowl
of fried chicken, eggs, several fruit pies, cakes, cookies, loaves of homemade bread, freshly churned but-
ter, a great comb of honey, and a whole pail of milk.

The lucky, lucky people! Little did they know, as they lay there asleep, what it was like here in war-torn Virginia.

The mists were now so thick he could hardly see a yard ahead of him. They seemed to be on a narrow, raised area, with the mist boiling up on one side. In time he discovered that he was on a dike along a canal. The dike had been blasted by cannon shell and was potted with holes, filled with water. Some of the weary soldiers, unable to see their feet, stumbled into the holes and sprawled flat. They floundered in slippery ooze and finally got up, sobbing in discouragement.

Len was startled by a horrible scream, followed by a splash. "Albert's fell in!" a man yelled.

Black shapes swarmed together at the canal edge. The ground there was crumbly. "Watch out!" someone shouted, but too late, for there was another splash as a second man went in.

Len threw himself down on the slimy ground and peered through the mist. He saw a hand come up. He reached for it. "Grab my feet! I've got him!" he yelled, as he struggled to hold on to the man, scrambling up out of the water. The mud was as slick as glass. Len could feel the man slipping back and pulling him toward the canal. "Help!" he screeched.

Someone seized his legs. Someone else reached for the man in the water and helped Len haul the dripping soldier to safety. A short distance away the second man who had fallen in was also rescued. They took off their clothes, and the rescuers did what they could to wring them dry.

"Albert, you sure could do with some hot coffee," a soldier said.

"Shut up!" Albert replied.

The men sighed. All of them could use hot coffee.

"Step out on the double-quick, Albert," one of the men advised, "else, in them wet duds, you're going to get noo-mony."

"Got it already," Albert mumbled, and coughed hollowly.

Oh, for some food! Len thought longingly. If ever I'm home again, I'll lick my plate clean every meal. Mamma'll never again have to say, "Don't waste food, Len."

They went on, the voices coming out of the mist and Albert complaining that he had the shakes he was so cold. Len's teeth were chattering. He was wet, too, from lying on the dike, hanging on to Albert. No one had thought to order Len to undress and wring out his clothes.

Oh, for a fire, he thought, and immediately longed more for food, then decided he wanted sleep even worse. "Aren't we ever going to stop?" he asked, but got no reply.

About noon they thankfully left the canal and the mist, and toiled along a road of red clay down which horses had passed, evidently while feeding, for there was a trail of corn grains that had dropped from their feed bags. Len was instantly on his knees, snatching them up, grain by grain, like a sparrow in a chicken yard. The grain wasn't too plentiful, but he filled half a pocket.

His fellow soldiers glanced at him uncomprehendingly, until they saw him clean the grain with water and then eat it. Suddenly twenty of them were down on the ground garnering. Len's source of supply was quickly gathered up.

He chewed his kernels, thankful his teeth were sound. He felt he got a little sustenance from them.

If only they'd pass an orchard with an apple or two left on the trees. There was little chance, however, for the area had been ravaged by the armies and was a waste of broken trees and fences, shelled houses, and burned areas.

"Why don't we get rations?" Len heard Albert ask querulously at the end of the long day.

"The Rebs captured our supply wagons," someone answered.

The troops were allowed to halt for fifteen minutes in an abandoned farmyard. Len immediately went into a shed, which had been a hen house. He poked into the straw to get stuffing for his good shoe, and found an egg. He brought it out triumphantly.

"Don't bust that egg near me!" a soldier said. "Man! Will it be rotten!"

Len wasn't so sure. Maybe the cold would have kept it fresh. It depended on how long it had been there. Albert was shivering and shaking nearby. "Want to try it?" Len asked.

The man shook his head, eyeing the egg, then said, "What would I lose? Guess I will at that." He took out an empty tin, broke the shell cautiously, then let out a pleased yelp. "It's good!" In an instant the egg was gone, and Albert was patting his stomach. "You're a real benefactor, fifer," he said.

Other soldiers dove into the hen house, but made no further finds. Len drew his belt up another notch, wishing he'd kept the egg for himself, but glad, too, that Albert, if anybody, had got it, for he needed it the most.

The bugles sounded, calling the soldiers back into formation. They listened unbelievingly. "It's night!" one man said. "They going to march us another whole night?"

Len was now so tired he could barely keep up with the army. For hours he hadn't seen any of his friends, Nat Jones, Bill Harrison, Jake Cooney, or Mr. Putnam. They had started off in the first ranks, which had left with Captain Hockness. Len realized he had been dropping behind without knowing it, and was in among the last of the troops. He hoped they'd reach a halting place before he collapsed and got left behind for good. He didn't see how he could keep going much longer.

But all night he managed to limp and stagger along, at times supporting himself with a stick, until the weight of it, light though it was, became a burden and he threw it away. It'll be forty hours without sleep and three days without rations by morning, he

told himself, and blinked, trying to keep his eyes
from closing.

When the next day dawned, the army had reached
a brown meadow, ringed with woods and backed by
a rise of ground that ended in a clifflike formation.
They were called to a halt. The men dropped to the
ground, their faces gray. They could hear artillery
in the distance. Evidently they were near a battle
area. They guessed that they would soon be engaged,
and they moaned. How were they to fight effectively,
feeling as they did now? They'd be licked before
they started.

But they were soon cheered, for a procession of
supply wagons came rumbling out of the woods. A
new issue of rations was given out. The men hastened
to build fires. Soon coffee was bubbling in the pots,
and the men were holding salt pork over the flames
and letting the drippings soak into their hardtack.
They ate and drank and smacked their lips as if they
had never tasted anything so good.

Len faced his biscuits without flinching, but was
glad that he found no trace of weevils when he
dipped them into his coffee. He fell asleep on the
ground the minute he finished eating.

# 16           BATTLE SMOKE

The soldiers had been in the meadow only three hours or so, when pickets came running into camp. Immediately bugles blew and drums beat. The trilling of fifes started up. The companies that had undergone the long sleepless march were reassembled.

Suddenly enemy fire swept over them. Shells whined as the enemy sought the range and rained his fire closer. The men were panicky, still so worn out from the past days' ordeal as to feel unable to cope with the Rebs.

An orderly shouted to Len to report to Captain Hockness to serve as aide. Len made a face. Now he'd be out of the main body. Because of having slept so long, he hadn't located any of his friends in the vast assemblage of men encamped in the meadow. He had hoped to march near them when they set off.

Today was going to be different in more ways than one. There'd be fighting as well as marching. Already the soldiers had been ordered into battle formation. The shelling was growing dangerous. Spurts of earth flew up here and there in the meadow. A man fell, moaning, and was hurried off by the hospital corps.

Len discovered that enemy cannon had been moved up into a fringe of woods above the meadow. He could hear the Rebs as they rammed down charges. They didn't seem to care how much noise they made. They even yelled defiantly. Then came a blast of light and a loud boom, as the cannon fired straight into the ranks.

He saw a great gap open among the men where the hit had struck. Instantly the army was on the move, the long lines advancing with guns at the ready. He saw the men kneel and fire as they went up the slope and into the fringe of trees. They reloaded as they went, and fired repeatedly when the gray-clad soldiers of the Confederate army became visible.

The Union ranks moved together at first, like stakes in a picket fence, with only a small space between each man. Then some of the stakes seemed to disappear. Len stared at foot-wide gaps, which spread to five-foot widths of bare ground, scattered over with men who had been shot. Some got up and staggered onward. Others stayed. Len realized these men would never move again.

The gaps in the ranks closed as the soldiers shifted toward each other and moved forward relentlessly, one line after another, to face the enemy. The men stepped over those who lay on the ground. They did not even look down at their comrades to see if they were badly hurt or dead. Those were the orders, Len remembered. Do not stop. Do not give aid. The soldiers had another job to do.

Len felt his throat tighten as he looked. Here he was, safe in the earthen breastworks with the captain and a few men, but his friends, including Mr. Put-

nam, were up there on the slope in a rain of fire. How
would they fare today, tired as they were and with
the Rebs so aggressive that they must know the Union
regiment's weakened state?

Before he could dwell miserably on his anxiety
the captain called him. The breastworks was halfway
up a hillslope, opposite a rise where the army was
advancing. At right angles to the breastworks was a
bluff, which rose high enough to look out over the
whole battle area. The captain told Len to go to the
bluff with a message for Colonel Losier.

Enemy artillery was still peppering the meadow,
although by now it was empty of men. The firing
would be directed into the trees before long. Len
must reach the bluff before the Rebs changed their
range.

He had barely set out, keeping among the trees,
when a bullet whisked past his head. It looked as if
a sniper had spotted him. He dodged behind the
thickest trunk he could find and waited to see if, indeed, he was being aimed at directly. Another bullet
flicked past, but the tree protected him.

He would have to take his chances by making

quick darts from tree to tree, so the sniper would miss him. For once he was glad he was small, for even a slender tree could protect him. He scampered out, dodging from shelter to shelter.

Suddenly a soldier stepped out from behind a large elm, his gun aimed directly at Len's chest. "Halt!"

Len all but fell to the ground in sheer fright, then steadied himself under waves of relief. The soldier was a sentry, one of his own company.

Len gave the password, and the sentry lowered his gun. "That fellow nearly got you." He jerked his head toward the place where Len had drawn the sniper's shots.

"Close," Len answered.

"He won't trouble no one no more," the sentry said. "We got *him!*" He told Len where to go next to find the sentry who would take him to Colonel Losier.

Soon he was trudging up a tree-covered slope that gradually grew steeper. He followed a second well-armed sentry. He felt safe and comfortable and rather thrilled at having passed through so much danger and been so close to enemy fire. At last he felt as if he'd become a real soldier, practically battle-scarred.

Jutting rocks furnished a superb lookout for the Northern army. Guards let Len pass, and the sentry went back to his post. As Len waited for the colonel to acknowledge him, he looked across the countryside, where continuous puffs of smoke and bursts of flame showed heavy fighting on distant slopes and in a valley.

There must be hundreds, perhaps thousands, of men engaged in the day's battle. He looked down toward the area where he thought the meadow lay, and wondered where Captain Hockness and the breastworks were. All of that area was covered with a smoke pall from the fighting. He could see nothing, but he could hear the dull boom of the cannon. The bluff seemed to be a sounding board for the roar of the artillery across from it. The noise was deep in tone, rapid and broken, coming in high frequency, as if the firing was paced at twenty reports a second. It was also like a tattoo played upon bass drums.

He wondered how the battle was going, and hoped fervently that this day would bring victory for the hard-pressed Yankees. They'd had many defeats in this area until now. The defeats had come only because the Rebs had had a better start, Len told himself. Surely the battles would turn in favor of the North before long.

The colonel was now free and was staring at him, so Len moved up with his message. The man sat at a table, loaded with maps and papers, a pistol, a pot of hot coffee, hard-boiled eggs, and three apples. While the colonel studied a map, Len eyed the apples, unconsciously licking his lips. He saw the colonel reach out, pick up an apple, and pause, holding it in the air. Then he glanced at Len and said, "Catch!"

Before Len realized what the colonel meant, the apple was flying toward him. He couldn't let a treasure like that go spinning off into space and crash against the rocky wall. He caught it, then wondered what he should do with it. Although the colonel had thrown it toward him, that didn't mean he intended Len to have it, just catch it.

"Alert," the colonel said to a captain, seated beside him. "I like them alert." To Len, he said, "Go ahead, soldier, eat it. Then help Private Maloy over there."

A little distance away Len saw a young soldier,

chopping the ends of stakes into points. Bundles of stakes still to be cut lay piled around him. Len munched his apple happily as he joined Maloy.

"Hatchet," mumbled the soldier, handing one to Len. "Make sharp points, to go in the ground easy." He turned his back on Len and went on doggedly chopping.

"What are they for?" Len asked.

Maloy seemed to be in a bad mood. He gave Len a sour glance and did not answer.

Len took his time about starting. He wanted to enjoy that apple to the last drop of juice. He ate the core and the stem and the seeds. All of it tasted delicious.

Maloy wheeled about. "Get going!" he said.

"What's the hurry?"

"Out there's the hurry!" Maloy pointed toward the smoke haze over the battleground. "They're out there waiting, as they've been waiting all these days, and the lists not brought in and nobody caring. Just me—I'm caring. I asked for this detail and for a helper, and they give me a boy like you—an apple-chawing boy, who doesn't care either!"

He chopped frantically, as if he meant to demolish

the pile by his side, but Len could see he was working carefully nevertheless. "What am I supposed to care about?" Len demanded, unable to understand the young soldier's insinuations. To his astonishment, he saw tears roll down Maloy's cheeks. "Doggone it! I care!" Len declared. "Whatever you're having fits about!" He tried to prove it by chopping vigorously.

Maloy rubbed his eyes and went on working. The flood of tears stopped. Len felt his weariness returning. All he'd done for the last few days was to put out energy and get none back. He was still short of food and sleep. If Maloy didn't still look so upset, he'd slow up on the chopping, but he felt his companion had a reason for wanting the work speeded. He couldn't guess what the stakes were for. They were too short for fencing. Besides, the army would hardly be making fences.

After Len's pile had grown quite large, Maloy faced him, looking more friendly. "Next we nail on the crosspieces," he said. "Then the colonel gives us the lists, and we paint. I guess by now you know what we're making."

"No, I don't."

"Grave markers, that's what."

Len felt as if his hair rose up and then lay down. Bundles and bundles and bundles of stakes were around them, actually hundreds of stakes, and they were grave markers. Now he understood. He chopped faster. He cared.

"I was in the shooting battle yesterday," Maloy mumbled, "beside my brother. He was killed."

No wonder Maloy was so moody. Len felt his companion's sorrow invade him. To have lost his brother was tragic. Len could think of nothing adequate to say, so he just chopped.

A guard came up and said, "Colonel wants you."

Len dropped the hatchet, vaguely noting big blisters on the palms of his hands. Maloy groaned. "Now they take you away, with all this here still to do!"

Len paused beside the colonel's telescope and stole a look through it. It was aimed at a distant road. What he saw shocked him. He placed himself before the officer, his face white.

"So you saw them," said the colonel. "Describe what you saw."

"A long, long line of wagons, moving slowly, with men walking beside them as if they hurt."

"Observant. I like them observant," the colonel said to the captain. "We'll send him back to Hockness. He'll be useful there. Now then, soldier, was that line enemy or Yankee?"

"I couldn't tell, sir. I had just a glance."

"It was our wounded, gathered up from yesterday's field. That wagon train of wounded is six miles long, young sir! Better steel yourself; you'll see something like that again." To the captain, he said, "Young codgers never think of that when they enlist. It's all glory and gunpowder." He shook his head, then addressed Len again. "Get back to Captain Hockness. Don't let yourself get caught. You're carrying a message in code. Swallow it if you're captured. Take an egg and another apple. Those are orders."

"Yes, sir." Len pushed the things into his ration kit, saluted, and followed the guard out.

He didn't feel like eating at the moment. It had been too upsetting to see that long line of wagons, with the walking wounded beside it, toiling along the road. The line was so long it seemed to go on forever. The colonel had said six miles long, which meant yesterday's casualties had been extremely heavy.

What was today's battle like? he wondered.
Would the Yanks be able to beat back the Rebs?
Would there be another wagon train tomorrow, as
long and as desolate-looking as this one?

The last sentry sent Len back in among the trees.
The firing in that area had tailed off. The artillery
seemed to be aimed in another direction now. He
ran along confidently, then was startled by a sharp
whistle. He darted behind a tree, crouched, and got
ready to spring upon anyone who showed himself.

"Soldier!" a voice called, then added a countersign, which Len knew he could accept. He ventured
out, a little cautious, but not worried. He saw a man
in the medical-corps uniform coming toward him.
"I'm Dr. Carrington. Can you take me to Captain
Hockness? My horse was shot, or I'd not be on foot."

"I'm going to him." Len led on, watching carefully for signs of snipers. He did not like the way people suddenly appeared before he was aware of them,
first the sentry and now the doctor.

The ground seemed more torn than he remembered it, and he wondered if he'd lost his way. Then
he saw some trees he recognized, and realized that
the enemy artillery had been splintering trees and

tearing up ground during his absence. He found a stone wall he had passed earlier. Up ahead should be the breastworks, but now he saw a flattened area in its place, with a scattering of sticks and rails. Only mounds were left of the earthen walls.

He grasped the doctor's arm. "The breastworks is gone! I don't see the captain or his men. I don't see anyone!"

"Stay here," the doctor said. He ran forward. Len saw him stop and bend over something behind one of the mounds. He straightened up, shaking his head.

Len would have run up to see, but was stopped by an odd wheezing sound. He listened. The noise was like heavy but painful breathing. He walked toward it.

In a hollow of torn earth lay Captain Hockness, trying to drag himself along the ground. A bloody trail showed he had been at this endeavor for some time. Len shouted for the doctor.

"Doctor!" the captain muttered groggily, but looked revived by the very word. "How'd a doctor get here?"

Dr. Carrington ran down the slope. With Len helping, he carried the captain to the stone wall. Here

Len gathered tree branches and foliage to form a refuge for the captain.

Captain Hockness told them that a cannonball had made a direct hit on the breastworks, killing all in its shelter except the captain himself, who had been thrown outside thirty feet or more with a badly cut leg. He also seemed to be suffering from concussion and wandered a bit as he talked, but otherwise he was all right, except for the pain.

The doctor made him as comfortable as possible under a shelter of boughs. Len crouched beside him to watch and help. Then, just as the doctor got his knife case and medical kit open for first-aid treatment, a sudden volley of firing burst out practically over their heads.

The doctor dove under the shelter and squeezed himself up close to the captain. There was no room for Len, so he tried to jump into a hollow of ground next to the stone wall. Before he made it, a soldier leaped over the wall, crashed into him, and sent him staggering downhill. He managed to keep on his feet, but could not stop, for suddenly he found himself surrounded by an avalanche of running soldiers.

They poured over the wall, yelling and waving

their muskets, and swept him along with them. They were an enemy contingent, and about the worst neighbors he could have. Len was in a fine pickle, a Yank soldier running with the enemy and with no way to stop or to save himself. He was likely to be knocked down and trampled underfoot if he even slowed up. Soon someone would discover his blue uniform and put an end to him.

They galloped through the trees like a forest fire. Soon Len's lungs felt ready to burst. He stumbled once or twice. He couldn't hold out much longer, he thought.

He saw a stump directly in his path. The men pressed so close to him on both sides that he knew he wouldn't be able to pass around the stump. Yet how was he to find strength to leap over it? It was too high. He was too spent.

He sucked in a great breath and threw himself into the air. He felt his feet clear the stump; then he hit the ground. The Rebel soldiers behind him, blocked likewise by the stump, were less tired than he, and simply floated over it and went racing on. No one noticed the exhausted, small Union soldier rolled up like a ball at the stump's base.

## 17                                LOST

The hurricane of men finally grew sparser and then ended. Len heard the pounding of their feet grow dimmer. Finally there was total silence. He did not move until then. Cautiously he peered about. Nothing stirred anywhere. He was alone in the wood and, what was better, it was growing dark. Soon the night would protect him. He didn't know where he was or where the captain and doctor might be. He felt as if he'd run for miles with the enemy soldiers.

Eventually he'd have to find his regiment, but not

just now. He didn't know where to go, anyway. All firing had ceased. The silence seemed almost as impressive as the thundering of the guns.

He stood up, rubbing his shins and arms. He felt so tired he wanted to crawl under a leaf and just stay there. He knew he must find a good place to spend the night. It was already cold, and by morning would be worse. If he found a road, he could follow it. Eventually it would lead to shelter. He would certainly not follow the Rebs; yet he wished he could locate a Union picket so as to report their passage. It might be important.

But where should he go? He decided to turn back the way he had been forced to run. Then he remembered how he'd got himself located when he'd served as a picket, so he painfully climbed a tree. Off to the right, perhaps two miles away, he saw a long line of yellow light from a fire, but not a campfire or a series of them. Since he couldn't figure out what it was, he decided he should cautiously investigate.

Although he lost sight of the flame once he was back on the ground, he went toward the smoke haze above it. At length he found himself at the edge of a stream, banked by willows. Across it he saw what was burning—the pine stringers of a railroad. The Yanks had evidently come that way and set the fire. Len knew they destroyed stretches of railway where they could, to keep the Rebs from getting needed supplies through.

He could feel the warmth in the air from the flames. The warmth drew him like a magnet. He waded the stream and was soon squatting beside the burning stringers, turning his back and then his face to the heat.

He got out his rations and pan and warmed up his meat. The colonel's hard-boiled egg was crushed in its shell, but was good anyway. He made coffee and ate the colonel's apple. Then he felt sleepy. He had lost his blanket when the Rebs came over the wall, but the fire would keep him warm. He glanced up at the sky, and decided it would not rain, so he could get along without shelter. He lay down where the warm air would blow over him and was soon asleep.

At dawn odd snorts awoke him. He discovered a soldier snoring beside him. Len started up in alarm, then saw that the man was a Yank. He examined the fire. The stringers had burned themselves out, leaving a glow of hot ashes, stretching along as far as Len

could see. Although the railroad had been laid with
old strap rail, and couldn't have been a very good
line, Len knew it was going to be a serious loss to the
Confederates when they tried to transport their ammunition.

He glanced at the sleeping Yank, feeling glad to
have him near. Heaven alone knew how he'd got
there, but it was almost certain he'd be able to tell
Len where to find his regiment.

There was no sound of shooting. Both armies were
probably at rest. He had no way of knowing where
friends or enemies were. He gathered up some brush
to start a breakfast fire over the hot coals. The smell
of his coffee reached the soldier, who sat up, then
swore loudly.

"You seen any horse?" he asked Len.

"Horse?"

"Had the rein around my wrist. Thought he
couldn't get loose without waking me. Now he's
gone. We got to find him, soldier. You go that way,
and I'll go opposite."

Len gathered up his breakfast, glad that he'd got
his tack toasted and his coffee made in time. He went
through the willow thicket downstream, eating as he

walked. Eventually he found fresh hoofprints in the mud, leading deep into the willows, where the horse's dangling reins had caught and were holding him fast.

A horse. How he liked them! Len patted the beast with enthusiasm. This one was friendly, and seemed glad to see him. Len disentangled the reins, mounted, and rode back to his campfire to wait for the soldier.

"I know where your outfit's at," the soldier said, as he gobbled his breakfast. "I'll take you along. I got drove off yesterday when the Rebs broke through. The horse pitched and bolted, screeching like a banshee, scared worse than any man I ever seen."

"How'd the battle go?" Len asked, his thoughts on his friends. He had been fretting over them in the back of his mind all the day before. Even when he'd been asleep, he'd felt a weight of anxiety. He hoped Mr. Putnam was safe. He wondered about Captain Hockness and the doctor, too, and hoped they hadn't been discovered and taken prisoner.

"It was pure butchery," the soldier answered. "I don't see how we're going to go on taking such losses. You should have seen the wagons full of wounded pass."

"I saw them."

"How're we going to hold up?"

"Maybe the Rebs are just as bad off."

"Could be, but just the same, there shouldn't be such losses. . . . Well, climb on! It's up to us to jump back into the fray."

They rode several miles, talking little, for both were dead tired. Len thought of home. It seemed like a dream he had had years ago. He tried to arouse his indignation by thinking of Mr. Thrace so that the thought of home would not be too pleasant and fill him with the longing to be there, but even Mr. Thrace seemed dreamlike. What Mr. Thrace had done seemed unimportant and far away, as if it had never happened. Compared with what was going on now, it was nothing. . . . Maybe he should have tried to like his stepfather. He guessed he had been pretty hard on Mr. Thrace. He hadn't thought of that before. Had he missed out on something at home? He remembered that Mr. Putnam had said, "I think it gives Dick something, too, to lean on—to have a substitute for his father." Len couldn't see himself leaning on Mr. Thrace, but still he could get a glimmer of how nice it would be if they were on good terms and if he liked the man.

Then he shrugged. Home was a dream. He mustn't think about it any longer. He was in the army, defending his country. If he felt heartsick, knowing his friends to be in danger, if he was cold, hungry, and tired, it was something he'd put himself into by enlisting, and through a lie at that. He had to take what came. It was too late now for regrets.

"I want to find Mr. Putnam," he said aloud, his lonesomeness showing in his voice.

Len and the soldier wandered around all day, riding toward the sound of artillery, then backtracking as their ears told them the battle area had shifted. The ground was torn with shelling. They saw abandoned equipment everywhere. Len found a blanket, and wrapped himself in it, not caring how he looked, anxious only to be warm for a change.

Finally at dusk they rode through a pass and came out into a valley, studded with shelter tents, fires, and clumps of soldiers. The ragged and grimy men were a welcome sight to Len. He had found his company. And his companion's cavalry unit was encamped a quarter of a mile beyond.

Len had to choke back his deep disappointment when he learned that both Mr. Putnam and Jake Cooney were out on picket duty. He noticed that many of the men were nursing minor wounds, but was told that his friends had escaped harm during the heavy fighting.

He did find Nat Jones. "It was rugged, Goober," he said. "It's a wonder we've got a man alive."

Roll call had revealed that many of the men who had made the long march together were missing. Fresh reinforcements had arrived, however, to help out when the next battle started.

"We've got cavalry holding our flank, and we've brought up cannon. Tomorrow might go better." Nat Jones didn't look confident, however. "Wish Putnam was around to play some of his tunes. They'd sound right nice tonight, when we're all so dismal."

Len jerked out his fife. Soon he had a crowd around him. It seemed queer to be playing gay songs like "The Money Musk," "Rover Quick Step," and "Old Dog Tray," when everyone looked so discouraged and worn out. He did not play Mr. Putnam's "Goober Galop," although he knew it well. It made him feel too lonesome for his friend that night.

The men hummed and sang. Their sorrowful faces cleared a little. They drifted off to their sleeping places, and Len curled up in his blanket, feeling strangely rested.

# 18       THE GOOBER GALOP

Next day Len was on the main battlefield. If he'd
thought yesterday that the meadow had been too full
of flying bullets for comfort, he now had to change his
opinion. Today the air contained so many missiles it
seemed to be raining them.

His cap was shot off, along with a tuft of hair, as a
bullet grazed his scalp. The light flesh wound bled
down over his face, making him look ghastly, although he did not know that at first, since he could
not see himself. Another bullet went through a fold in

his jacket sleeve, leaving a hole with a burned edge. He shivered. A little closer, and he'd have had a crippled arm.

He was piping signals near one of the drummers. The smoke from the discharges rose around them and made their eyes sting. The noise was enough to burst their eardrums. He found himself stumbling over men in his path, and gasped in dismay. They were wounded soldiers. He was stepping on them before he saw them. He wanted to stop and apologize, but no one was allowed to stop. The orders had been repeated that morning. "Do not stop! Do not give aid!" All he could do was try to jump over the men who had fallen on the field.

He was on the run for what seemed like hours. Suddenly the booming of cannon started. He saw the ground rise up as if a dynamite charge had been let loose under the advancing men of his company. Many were killed.

Enemy artillery rained a lethal fire, making the army swing to the left. Yank artillery answered. Yank cannon roared. The Rebel fire weakened, then came back full force. The Yanks had turned again, only to confront the enemy on a hillslope. For a time it was hand-to-hand fighting. The bayonets were deadly in their work.

For a while the Union army pushed uphill, forcing the Rebs to retreat. Then suddenly, when they felt they were going to win a sure victory, they heard loud, defiant yells. They looked up to see an unending line of Confederates rise from hidden positions on the ridge above them and start down, firing as they came. The Southern artillery adjusted its aim, and Minié balls came down as thick as bees in swarm. The Yank army could not hold. With a sinking heart, Len heard the order for retreat.

After that, it was a shambles. He ran. The whole regiment ran. It seemed as if they were running in disorder. Len couldn't tell. All he knew was that they rushed over the battlefield with the enemy in murderous pursuit.

Then Yank reinforcements swirled in around the fleeing troops. The Northern and Southern armies switched back and forth fighting each other hand to hand. Something hit Len on the head and he fell, stunned.

When he came to himself, the battle was raging across the valley in a wood. His head felt woozy, but

he could find no wound, just a welt on his forehead.
He could hardly bear to look around him, there were
so many fallen men from both armies strewn over the
field, bundles of inert blue and gray. He staggered to
his feet and hastened toward the fighting, as a few
other soldiers who had been able to pull themselves
together were doing.

Len had covered several rods when he discovered
the soldier, Albert, on hands and knees, trying to
crawl off the field. He was wounded in the back, Len
couldn't tell how badly.

Albert looked up at him. "Your friend Putnam's
back there. Saw him fall."

Len swayed as if he, too, had been shot. Mr. Putnam wounded? Maybe dead? His best friend—the
man he turned to as he would have to his father—
here, in all this horror, with no one to help him!
Len forgot the army orders about stopping on the
field. But here was Albert, too, wounded and bleeding. He should try to do something for the man.

"Go find him, kid," Albert said. "Him and me had
a talk. We was on picket duty with Cooney last night.
If Putnam's alive, he needs to see your face again. Go
on. Never mind army orders."

"But you—you, too!" Len didn't want to wait now to help Albert; yet he felt like a monster, deserting him.

"Go on! I can still crawl. *He* can't."

On hearing this, Len rushed back across the field and scanned each fallen man as he went. Where was he to find Mr. Putnam? The field was acres wide, and there were several hundred men prone upon it. How could he trace him? It would be impossible to examine each one there.

He moaned and called piteously, "Mr. Putnam! Mr. Putnam!" yet he knew that his voice would not carry far under the roar and cracking of cannon and musketry. Men stirred as he went by. Some begged him to stop. One asked for water, but because it was not Mr. Putnam, he went stonily past, feeling heartless. He had to find Mr. Putnam. He just had to. He thought of the things his friend had done for him— mended his sox, bought him useful articles, played games, taught him to play the fife.

The fife. Len clasped his shaking hands together. The fife! Mr. Putnam's fife! It was safe in his inner pocket. Len could call to him with it. Its shrill piping would carry to him. Mr. Putnam would recognize its note, especially if Len played their very own tune, "The Goober Galop." What matter if the "Galop" was a tune for dancing and joy, and that this was a field of sorrow and misery. If Mr. Putnam heard it, he would know Len was looking for him, and he would find a way, somehow, to let Len know where he was.

So Len raised the fife and trilled, turning left and right as he played, in order to see the whole field. Amazed faces lifted among the wounded. Moans and groans rose up, as if in resentment that anyone should play a galop in the midst of so much agony.

Len played his tune over and over, and walked across the field, watching tensely for a sign of response. Finally he saw a white rag or handkerchief wave feebly. He hurried toward the place, playing hopefully. The cloth flapped again and fell to the ground. He was sure that the hand that had signaled so weakly belonged to his lost friend. He rushed over and threw himself beside the tall, thin man on the ground. He wept with joy.

Mr. Putnam was deathly pale and hardly able to speak. He'd been wounded in the head and breast, and was apparently very weak, but a light came into his eyes as he looked at Len. "My Goober's galop sounded good," he whispered with great effort. Then he moaned under a wave of pain.

Len felt terrified. Was he to find his friend only to have him die? He gently touched the man's cheek. "My ch-ch-children," Mr. Putnam said. "Take them my wallet, Len. Promise."

"Yes, of course," Len answered. He carefully unbuttoned Mr. Putnam's jacket and drew out the packet he found inside, enclosed in its rubber pouch. Mr. Putnam watched attentively as Len put the packet into his own breast pocket. Then he smiled and closed his eyes.

Len waited despondently, wondering if there was anything he could do. If only he knew how to tend his friend's wounds or get him off the battlefield or get a doctor to him. If only he had Dr. Carrington along now. But he was helpless and ignorant and useless, and his friend was in desperate straits.

Suddenly a hand seized his shoulder. Len sprang up, startled nearly out of his wits. He found himself face to face with Jake Cooney.

"You lunatic, Goober!" Jake said. "You and your galop. So that's how you found him!" He knelt and examined Mr. Putnam. "I think maybe he's fainted.

Goob, you've got to git! The Rebs are coming back
this way. You mustn't be caught. You ain't wounded
—at least not bad—so you've got to save your hide
while you can."

"No!" said Len, with a frantic gesture toward Mr.
Putnam.

"Go on. I'll look after Putnam."

"I won't leave him."

"You got to. You're disobeying orders."

Mr. Putnam opened his eyes. "Take my wallet . . . to my ch-children," he said, giving Len a
worried look.

"I don't want to leave you," said Len pleadingly,
but although the man looked glad, he also looked
anxious.

Jake said, "Goober, do what he wants. Don't cross
him. He's very low. I'll stay with him. The Rebs will
grab you if you don't hurry. They won't touch the
wounded, so he'll be safe from them, and later the
hospital corps will pick him up—pick us both up.
I'm wounded, too. I've had it in the arm and one
foot. Go on, Goob! Save yourself, and that way you
can save us both, if there's any chance for us."

Len could say no more when it was put that way.

He pressed Mr. Putnam's hand, and pushed his canteen and rations into Jake's. He undid his blanket and would have spread it over Mr. Putnam, only Jake pushed him away.

"Get going, Goober, I'll do that! You'll just make it before the Rebs come in sight. I can tell from the popping of the guns that there's no time to lose. Go up that rise. Then drop through the brush to the river. It's up to you after that."

# 19            THE HOSPITAL

Len wandered for two days before he found his regiment again. Stray Reb units blocked him, no matter what direction he chose. Often he had to lie low in thickets and wreckage. It grew so cold he dared not stay quiet long. He felt weak from lack of food. Finally he found a Yankee outpost, and was told where to go.

His first act back in camp was to inquire about Mr. Putnam, Jake Cooney, and Albert. Albert was on the hospital list, and had been removed from the field with the other wounded. Mr. Putnam and Jake had been reported as missing in action. That could mean captured by the Confederates or dead. There seemed to be no trace of either of them.

When the death lists were posted, Len searched them anxiously. The names of his two friends did not appear. This left him a faint hope.

He requested permission for a furlough, because he wanted to keep his promise to Mr. Putnam and take his wallet to his children. On the same day a new death list was posted. Men listed as missing in action were now listed as dead, for by now the enemy had removed their wounded and dead from the field, and had carried off some wounded Yanks as prisoners. However, they had not turned in the names of Putnam or Cooney. Both of Len's friends were very likely dead, it would seem from this, and had been given up by the Northern army.

Len's furlough came through, and he left immediately for Washington. There he would report to headquarters and then journey to Germantown on his errand to the children.

He kept thinking mournfully of Mr. Putnam, then of his poor children, who were now indeed orphans and would have to remain in the home until they were grown. He wondered what he could say or do to comfort them. If only he could take his mother along! She'd gather them close and soothe them. She'd know how to make them feel less alone and unhappy.

In Washington he examined the names on the room directory in the headquarters building to see where he should report. He was surprised to find the name of Emily Jane's father posted on it. So he had an office in the building. Len had almost forgotten that Judge Leonias Bradford existed. Nor had he thought of Emily Jane. She was living in Washington now, he recalled, but he wouldn't look her up. He didn't want to take the time. Mr. Putnam's children came first.

As he handed his furlough paper out to be stamped, the corporal at the desk said, "Got a dispatch for you, Baldwin. Sent back from Camp X. Been here three days."

Len took it wonderingly, and read with crawling flesh, "Will Baldwin, Steward, 31st Sec., A Battalion, Hospital Corps D, wounded in action. Transferred, Washington, St. Barnabas Hospital."

His brother Will wounded! Len tottered on his feet. How badly? Where was Will? He could hardly assimilate the facts, his head whirled so. Finally he calmed down. Will was close. Actually right here in the city. Len could look up the hospital, find him, see for himself.

He dashed from the room and down the hall, and was tearing out of the building when he remembered he must ask where St. Barnabas Hospital was located. He saw a groom helping a young lady, wearing a fur-trimmed bonnet, a fur tippet, and a blue velvet coat, get out of a carriage. He was approaching the man to ask his question when the young lady cried, "Why, Len Baldwin! It's you!"

It was Emily Jane.

She sprang toward him, put her gloved hands on his shoulders, and stood staring, with eyes that grew wide in horror. "Len!" Her voice trembled. She seemed deeply shocked. "You're little! And so thin! Why, you look like a poor little plucked chicken."

"Well, I'm not!" Len blazed, tossing his head. For an instant he forgot Will and his anxiety over him, and Mr. Putnam and his sorrow over him. Then it was all back on him again. He jerked away from her. "My brother's been shot. I've got to go to him. Do you know where St. Barnabas Hospital is?"

"Indeed I do, Len," she answered. Now she was grave, as if she understood how upset he was, and perhaps saw still more, for she looked him up and down, her eyes taking in his scalp wound, his torn and grimy uniform, his thin face with purple circles under his eyes, his ragged sox showing through holes in his shoes, one of which was larger than the other. Len had no idea at the moment how he looked.

"Len, dear boy," she said softly. "Don't you worry about a thing. I will drive you to the hospital this minute." She climbed briskly into her carriage. He followed. "I will help you all I can. Is your brother injured badly?"

"I don't know."

"I feel very sorry."

Len hung his head, too sad to talk. All he wanted was to get there. She seemed to realize this, and kept the horse at a swift pace. She did not question him anymore, but her eyes were troubled. She let him down at the entry and said she'd wait for him, and that he might ask her for any service she could give.

Soon he was in a large crowded ward of wounded soldiers. He squeezed his way down a narrow aisle between countless beds, as well as mats of wounded men on the floor. Somewhere among all the moaning, delirious, desperately wounded soldiers he would find Will. He could hardly believe that his lively stalwart brother, who had enlisted in the war to care for others, was now flat on his back in a place like this.

At last he saw him, his head propped up slightly by a wad of cloth. He was covered with a torn blanket, and had no sheet in this unheated, wintry room. His face was flushed, as if he had a fever, but his eyes shone when he saw Len.

"Good heavens, boy! What are you doing here?"

Len grasped Will's hands and pressed them fervently. "Are you hurt bad?"

"My leg's gone," Will answered matter-of-factly, "but I'm lucky at that. I'm alive. I'll get me a peg leg. If it had been my arm—"

"Your leg?" Len's voice broke. He could hardly bear it that Will had lost his leg. He thought of how Will used to run over the lawn, playing catch with him, and how he used to skate with him in the winter. Now—

"Don't take it to heart. It won't stop me. I can still be a doctor someday. When this heals, I'll apply for a clerkship in the hospital-supply headquarters of the army. I'll still be helping."

"Yes, but how are you feeling?" Len demanded worriedly, for his brother looked ill.

"Fair." He winced as he spoke. "I have pain. I suppose there's no escaping pain. Some of these other fellows are plain out of their heads with it." He glanced at the nearest cot. "Like *him!*" His eyes grew sorrowful. "There aren't enough doctors. That's what's wrong. Or nurses. And no one to wash up and make beds. Not enough bedding, and it's winter. There isn't even proper food or enough cooks. This war's all wrong." He trembled as a wave of pain swept over him. "They brought us off the battlefield in a train of bumping wagons—a train six miles long."

"Six miles!" Len exclaimed. "I saw it!" He stared in horror at his brother. It had never occurred to him that someone he knew, or who was close to him, was in that gruesome train.

He noticed Will's attention shift to something across the room. The moaning about them seemed to lessen for a minute. One or two oh's rose faintly from the cots.

"Who's that, I wonder," said Will.

Len glanced over his shoulder, to discover Emily Jane sailing through the ward like a blue boat between the wrinkled brown blankets. She stopped at the foot of Will's cot.

"Sir, may I introduce myself," she said to Will. "I am Emily Jane Bradford. Your brother Len is my pen companion. I do hope, sir, that you are not suffering too badly."

"I am pleased to meet you," Will said politely, but the words came from drawn lips.

"I met your brother up home. He saved my life from a runaway horse," she said hurriedly, as if wishing to occupy him, so he would not feel the pain so much. "He was very brave. In fact, I think it was his courage that fooled me. I've been thinking that he was quite big—much taller and older looking. Now that I see him again he seems pitifully small and young to be wearing that soldier's uniform."

"He is," Will answered. "That's what he is most certainly!"

"I'm not," Len mumbled.

"You're thin as a picked crow," Will said. "I'll bet you've been sick."

"No, I'm fine. It's just that we didn't get much rations lately."

"I could skin the man alive who dragged you into this war," Will snorted.

"Sir!" Emily Jane said with sudden fire in her eyes. "My father, Judge Leonias Bradford, arranged Len's acceptance into the United States Army as a soldier."

"He must have been out of his mind," Will exclaimed, his pain forgotten behind his indignation. "The idea of putting a twelve-year-old boy into the army."

"Twelve!" she cried. "He's not twelve. He's fifteen. He said so."

Four eyes focused on Len. He looked up, then his gaze fell before their grim stare.

"Did you lie to her?" Will asked.

"Yup," Len mumbled.

"Len!" Emily Jane exclaimed. "You have misrepresented the truth!"

"Call it a lie," said Will, and there was a faint smile on his lips. "So she thought you were fifteen and told her father, and that's how you worked it. I assure you, I've wondered."

"I am very angry with you," Emily Jane said fiercely. "My father, Judge Leonias Bradford, is a man of integrity. He wishes to have a good name, like our noble president, who is called Honest Abe. Now what will people think when it is known that my father supported a lie in this fashion, and used his influence to get a liar into the army? I am very, very angry!" Her voice broke. "And disappointed, too." She wiped a tear from her eye.

"Don't," Will said, looking more disturbed by her tear than by her anger. "I'm sorry my little brother has upset you."

Little! thought Len, then shrugged. What did it matter? He'd been too busy to grow and had had too little to eat and too little sleep. He'd lost his best friend, and found his brother wounded, and still must visit Mr. Putnam's bereaved children and talk to them about their father. What did it matter that Emily Jane and Will said he was little or too young to be in the army? He was in it, and had served his country as best he could. He was sorry he'd cheated to get in. But what did it matter now what they said?

"I will forgive him," Emily Jane declared. "He did not realize." She smiled reassuringly at Will, then lifted up a small watch, hanging from a gold chain around her neck. "I must rejoin my father. In fact, I had gone to drive him home when I encountered Len. Father must be wondering where I am. . . . Len," she continued, "I am distressed by your appearance. I am afraid that army life has not been good for you. You are much changed. I feel so strange when I look at you. It actually seems as if you have shrunk."

"I can't have," Len said. "You're silly."

"I am still at your service, should you need me," she answered, ignoring his personal comment. She gave Will her hand to shake. "Good-bye, Mr. Baldwin. I shall inquire how you are, and send in some fruit. I do hope your health will improve."

Will looked after her admiringly as she walked in a dignified manner past the cots. "Isn't she pretty?" he said.

"She said she was distressed by my appearance," Len growled. "If she could see my nits, she'd be more than distressed." He scratched.

"Poor kid," Will said. "You bit off more than you could chew, and I guess you realize it deep down, but if I know you, you'll never admit it." He patted Len's shoulder. "You're one of the best. By the way, Mr. Thrace is coming. He sent word the minute he heard I was wounded. He should get here tonight."

"Mr. Thrace?" Len felt surprise. Then he felt gladness, for he was worried about Will. He didn't want to leave his brother, yet knew that he would have to if he were to see the Putnam children. He didn't feel as if he should give up his errand to them after his promise to Mr. Putnam. But how could he both stay and go? Before long his furlough would run out, and he'd be obliged to leave Will behind alone. It helped solve the problem to hear that Mr. Thrace was coming.

He told Will about the young Putnams and explained how he happened to be on furlough.

"You go to them," Will said at once. "Leave today. I'll be all right, and Mr. Thrace will soon be here to keep me company. I'm lucky—we're both lucky—to have such a good stepfather. He comes right along when you need him."

"Maybe," said Len, feeling his face grow red. He wasn't sure if Will was right about Mr. Thrace or not. He still wasn't sure.

"Go find out about the train schedule now," said Will. "I feel very tired after all this visiting, and would just as soon sleep. Why don't you take the first train out and get this job over with? You owe it to those kids."

Len left, much eased in his mind. In another hour he was on a train, rattling its way northward.

## 20          THE ORPHANAGE

When Len reached Germantown, he stopped at an inn long enough to bathe and have his clothes washed, ironed, and mended by the maids while he waited in his room. He still looked shabby in his worn uniform, but he was clean and no longer itched. He felt ready to present himself as Mr. Putnam's friend to the lonely children.

He wished he could have brought Will along. This seemed more like a job for a man than for himself. It would be an even better job for Mr. Thrace than for Will. Mr. Thrace was nearer Mr. Putnam's age. What did a fellow Len's age say to lonely orphans?

At the orphanage he was taken into a high-ceilinged, unheated, and poorly furnished parlor. A tall sour-faced woman, the matron, Mrs. Snipe, sniffed at him and said, "The Lord help us if this is the kind of soldiers we Northerners have!"

Len found Mr. Putnam's children just as forlorn-appearing as he had expected. In his presence Mrs. Snipe coldly told them their father was dead and that this soldier friend had come to see them.

The little girl was too young to take in the bad news, but the boy nearly went into a convulsion of grief. He shook from head to foot, turned deadly pale, and could hardly breathe. As he grew calmer, Len could see that he fought with himself to keep back tears, as if he thought tears were sissy and that Len, a boy near his age, would look down on him. It was only when Len brushed tears away from his own eyes that Dick cried. Then he cried hard. Lucy squeezed against him and wailed loudly, still not realizing how sorrowful the news was. Len waited until Dick's desolate sobbing ended, then gave him the rubber-wrapped packet he'd brought.

He was surprised to see the boy take out the two boats and the doll, which he had carved as presents for the children. He had not known that they were inside. He couldn't imagine how Mr. Putnam had managed to keep them during the long march and the terrible battles he'd been in, or why he had even wanted to. It made his heart ache to think Mr. Putnam had cherished them to that extent.

At this moment the boats did not interest Dick much, but Lucy snatched up the doll and clung to it as if she'd never let it go.

Len was shocked when Dick opened the next part of the package. It contained Mr. Putnam's identification papers. Len knew little about business or military regulations, but he felt that Mr. Putnam should have kept the papers on his person. He had been suffering too much to think clearly, so had handed them over. However, Len felt that if by some chance he had survived, he would need them. On the other hand, if he had died of his wounds, the papers would be needed by the military department to certify his death.

Len explained all this to Dick, and the boy gave them back. "I'll show them to my brother," Len promised. "He'll know what to do. He's in the army, too."

Len had planned to stay two or three days to try to cheer the children up, but next day, when he returned, Mrs. Snipe said, "Don't hang around here after today, young man. Them Putnams might as well get used to being total orphans, like any others here. It don't help to have you around listening to their carryings on."

Len looked at her angrily. "I know of no carryings on."

"Bawling and sniveling. Raising hob, too. I'll not have it after today!" She marched out of the room with a nasty stare at him over her shoulder.

Len clenched his fists. "I'll bet they didn't raise hob." He felt pity for the children. To think that they were in such a horrible place and in the care of such a mean woman.

As he rode back to Washington he kept thinking about them. No wonder Mr. Putnam had felt sad when he'd had to put his children into an orphanage, where no one would love them. Now that he was gone and could no longer check the situation by an oc-

casional visit or send money for their support, Mrs.
Snipe might even be cruel to them.

Len pondered a long time, wondering if there was
anything he could do. His thoughts wandered to
Will, but Will was wounded. Len couldn't give him
any problems while he was laid up. Maybe he should
discuss the problem with Mr. Thrace. He would still
be in Washington when Len got there. For Mr. Putnam's sake, he felt he could forget his cold attitude
and discuss this with his stepfather.

Len began to think of Mr. Putnam's remarks on
one of the last nights they had camped together, and
remembered how he'd questioned him and sounded
him out about Mr. Thrace. Dick had worshiped his
stepfather, Len had noticed. He had shown it by his
grief and by ways in which he unconsciously imitated
some of Mr. Putnam's gestures, such as tugging at a
forelock or pursing his lips in a funny little way.

Mr. Putnam had thought Len should have tried to
like Mr. Thrace, or at least tried to see some good in
him. They would both have been happier, Len ad-
mitted to himself cautiously. Now, if they were good
friends, he could say to his stepfather, "Help me help

those kids." He wondered if he dared say it anyway. In his heart of hearts he felt that if he asked such a thing, Mr. Thrace would not fail him.

He hurried to the hospital from the train, anxious to see if Will was better. The ward was as crowded as ever and as tragic. Men sobbed in pain. Some were in such agony they screamed repeatedly; some were so spent they called piteously for their wives or mothers, whom they would never see again.

Len found a stranger on Will's cot.

"My brother! Where's my brother?"

No one seemed to know. He went frantically from cot to cot, searching. But Will was gone. Had he died while Len was away?

Len staggered blindly out of the room. He groped his way toward the office, where only one person was in charge, trying to cope with the endless registry of the wounded and to keep charts and records. A staff of fifty people should have been there. Many nurses should have been on duty, too, but Len glimpsed only one or two.

A man entered the office behind him, and cried, "Oh, there you are!" Arms went around him, turning him about. He found himself staring up at Mr. Thrace.

Len was so stricken with anxiety over Will that he began to sob. He put his head against Mr. Thrace's broad chest and gulped, while tears rolled down his cheeks.

"There, there," his stepfather said, and his warm voice held the same comforting tone that Len's mother's would have held. "Will is much, much better. That young lady has moved him to her home."

Len's sobs stopped instantly. He looked into the man's face with joy and relief.

"I've been waiting here since train time to catch you when you arrived," Mr. Thrace said, "but missed you somehow. I knew you'd be anxious."

"Thank you," said Len. He gulped again. His stepfather had certainly never been more kind. "How'd you know I'd get in today?"

"I didn't, but I've been coming here every day about the time the train gets in from Pennsylvania. I'd have come tomorrow, too, to look for you. I knew you'd come here first."

"He's better?" Len hardly dared believe it yet.

"I should say so. I never saw such a change. I think your Emily Jane must have some magic. Being in her care has brought Will back on the road to recovery. No fever at all now."

Mr. Thrace had put his arm lightly across Len's shoulders, as if ready to draw away if Len showed the least annoyance at such familiarity. Len did not move. He was whirling inside with mixed emotions—gladness over his brother, gratitude to Mr. Thrace for coming to him, worry over Mr. Putnam's children, and an uncomfortable feeling that Mr. Thrace was better than he'd thought and that it was time to say so and make amends.

But he was bothered by the thought that he wanted to dump his problem on Mr. Thrace. He had been unfriendly to the man, yet now expected him to do him a favor. It didn't seem fair to ask, unless he could like him first.

So he stood there, wishing he could talk to him as he would have to Mr. Putnam. Then he thought, It's not for myself. Why should I hold back from asking for help for someone else, for the kids? He's not mean. He's never been mean. I feel it now. Then he thought, with a start of surprise, Why didn't I feel that way before about him?

He turned, so he faced Mr. Thrace. "I have a big thing to ask," he said, looking into the brown eyes to watch for the least sign of unfriendliness to show. As he started, there was only interest and sympathy apparent. "Those kids are in a terrible place. Do you suppose—I mean—could you—?"

He shook his head. He couldn't get it out. It was too big a favor, this wild idea he'd had. He hadn't liked his stepfather. He'd let him know that only too many times. He hadn't been decent at all. How could he ask what he wanted to ask?

"Your friend's children are in an orphanage," Mr. Thrace said, as if to prod him into continuing.

"Yes, sir."

"And you'd like to get them out, wouldn't you?"

Len couldn't answer. Mr. Thrace bowled him over the way he had guessed his thought.

"You would like to ask me if I would help."

"Yes, sir."

"You even want to go farther, but don't quite dare. Please, Len, don't let things of the past interfere.

Do you want to ask if I will take these children into our home? Is that what you want to ask?"

"Yes, Mr. Thrace," Len said humbly.

"I think that's a splendid idea, Len. I was hoping you'd suggest it." Mr. Thrace patted his shoulder approvingly.

"We should ask Mamma, too," Len said.

"We will—you and I."

"Yes. You and I," Len repeated. He clenched his fists. Here he was, saying "you and I" naturally. He didn't feel mad or suspicious or anything. It was as if the man was a friend and always had been.

Had he been? And Len had not seen it?

Len tried to recall his wrongs. His stepfather had scolded him, sometimes punished him. He had ordered him to go to school regularly. What was wrong with that, after all? He was just trying to act like a real father.

Len scowled, deep in thought, battling to sort things out. He's all right, he finally decided, not a snoop, not a tyrant. I guess that's what Mr. Putnam was trying to show me.

He swallowed hard then, wishing Mr. Putnam could know. He'd be pleased.

# 21    EMILY JANE MEDDLES AGAIN

On Will's advice, Len took Mr. Putnam's papers to the War Office before he left Washington. He was in a base camp a few days later, wondering why he had not yet been sent ahead to his unit on the battlefields, when he was called to the colonel's tent. He supposed the summons concerned Mr. Putnam's papers. However, he was never more shocked in his life than when he opened the document that was handed to him. He was being dismissed from the United States Army.

"No!" he exclaimed, and stamped the ground in

protest. "They can't dismiss me. I'm a regular en-listed soldier. They can't put me out."

He stormed up to the colonel and demanded an explanation.

The colonel was a huge man, who would have made four Lens. He seemed to find Len's anger funny, and laughed heartily. "Well, sir, my little fighting cock, it looks as if you've got big ideas, but it seems you're only twelve years old, and got into this war by illegitimate strategy, which we don't stomach from anyone that age. So we're putting you out."

"Please, sir. I've been a good soldier. I've been in battle."

"A battle is no place for kids. It's bad enough when they're blasted out of their homes in the towns that we shell." He glared at Len's pleading face, then added a little more gently, "Sorry, young sir. You're out and there's no appeal. When you're of age you might try again."

The colonel turned away. Len knew there was nothing more to be done.

He went back to his tent to gather his things to-gether and report back to Washington. He felt terribly depressed, even disgraced, because he was put out. His name was in the mud. He shouldn't have lied about his age. But then, if he hadn't cheated to get in, he'd never have got into the army or known Mr. Putnam or had any of the exciting experiences he'd had. He brooded all the way to Washington and to the headquarters building.

He wondered why Mr. Thrace had told on him finally and got him dismissed. As his guardian, he could do that. Probably the temptation had been too great. He had always wanted Len to remain at home. Len did not feel angry at his stepfather, as he would have in the old days. He just felt sad, because it had happened.

He signed the final release papers at headquarters, then walked dolefully down the hall. He passed the office door with the name, Judge Leonias Bradford, upon it, and stared at it a moment, thinking about the man. What a lot of changes Emily Jane's father had made in Len's life—a man he had never even seen!

He walked on. He'd hire a hack and go out to see Will, then he guessed he'd head home. He wouldn't mind seeing home again. Soon the Putnam kids would be there, and that would be nice, but he wondered what he was going to do with himself now. It wouldn't seem right at all to be doing nothing about the war, when the fighting was still going on.

He looked up to discover Mr. Thrace coming through the outer door. "Why, hello!" He looked considerably surprised to see Len.

"Why did you hook me out of the army?" Len demanded, a little of his old indignation in his voice. Realizing this, he tempered it down. "I'd have liked it better, sir, if you'd talked it over with me first."

"Hooked out? Do you mean dismissed?" Mr. Thrace looked puzzled, then extremely pleased.

"Yes," Len answered. "Kicked out, in other words."

"How did it happen?"

"You ought to know. You told them my age."

Mr. Thrace put his hand over his mouth as if to poke back a laugh. He didn't look as embarrassed as he should have, Len thought, at having caused his dismissal and then been found out.

He said, "Come talk to Emily Jane. She just drove me here."

They went along together silently, Len trying to

hold back his hurt that the man he'd finally accepted as a friend and father had betrayed him to the army.

"This boy's been dismissed," Mr. Thrace said briefly to Emily Jane.

"Well, thank goodness, Len!" Emily Jane said in her usual quick way. "Now the record is clear, and my father, Judge Leonias Bradford, need no longer blush with shame to think he made such a mistake as to put you into the army. He was devastated emotionally when I told him your true age and how you'd deceived us both. He took steps immediately to have you dismissed, for he did not want *his* name on your papers any longer. He is a man of integrity."

"Len did not personally ask your father for his backing. It was you, who offered help through him." Mr. Thrace sounded stern. "Remember that, Emily Jane. It was you who started the ball rolling. You should not be so hard on Len. He is much upset by this."

"Oh dear," she exclaimed. "You are right. I *do* remember that I started things. I guess I was very wrong." She sighed, looking contrite, the way she had looked the day she'd swept Len away in her carriage long months ago.

Len felt extremely cross with her. What a meddler she was! Then, as her lovely blue eyes continued to seek a look of forgiveness, he smiled a little and shrugged. "At least I served for a while," he said. He glanced at Mr. Thrace gratefully for having defended him after Emily Jane had blamed him. For the first time since his dismissal he felt like lifting his chin and looking the world in the eye.

"We'll find you a way to go on serving the nation," his stepfather said. "I hear they need musicians for the band at home to play in the recruitment parades."

Len's eyes brightened. He hadn't thought of that possibility.

"For heaven's sake! Tell him your news!" Emily Jane cried.

"Yes indeed, yes, yes. It's about your friends, Len. They've been found. Both Putnam and Cooney. Both alive."

"How? How? Oh, is it really true?" Len was hardly able to stand the flood of joy that went over him. It was as if a thousand fifes had suddenly begun to trill and toot and sing—and, of course, it was "The Goober Galop" that hummed merrily through it all. "Tell me!"

"The two Union soldiers turned up in Libby Prison, and are held by the Confederates. Both are badly wounded, but are recovering. After you sent Putnam's papers in, they were found and identified. Cooney's papers were lost, too, for some reason."

Len's face fell. "But in Libby Prison? That's awful. Everyone says Libby Prison is next to dying."

"Tell him what *I* said." Emily Jane poked Mr. Thrace with a blue umbrella she was carrying.

"*You* tell him," Mr. Thrace answered.

"*I* said," she declared, emphasizing each word with a dramatic pause, "that I would tell my father, Judge Leonias Bradford, about your friends and their plight. And I did, too. My father knows some of the military leaders in the highest ranks of the United States Army. He also knows some of the Confederate leaders. Once before the war he dined at a banquet in the company of General Robert E. Lee himself. In other words, he knows influential people. Len, sometimes prisoners are exchanged between the two armies, so when I told my father last night about your friends, he said he would try to get them out of Libby Prison in the next prisoner exchange. I am sure he will succeed, because my father has proved time after time that he can succeed in anything. Isn't that so?"

Len was speechless. They were alive, those two friends he missed so, and now this girl felt she could rescue them through her father. He wondered if he dared hope. He saw Mr. Thrace nod. His stepfather believed Jake Cooney and Mr. Putnam could be saved. He felt a tight place in his throat relax. If Mr. Thrace was sure, then he, too, could be sure.

"There's a last piece of news," Mr. Thrace said, and now Emily Jane turned very pink. "There's going to be a wedding in the family."

"Who?" Len exclaimed in bewilderment. "Not Edie! Oh, I want Edie home."

"Will," Mr. Thrace said. "He's going to get married."

"Will!" Len cried. "Who'd marry *him?*"

"*I* would, Len Baldwin!" Emily Jane cried. "And what a dreadful remark to make about such a dear, noble young man—to imply that nobody would marry him. He has asked me, and I have said yes."

She smiled at him giddily, her eyes bright and blue and ashine with happiness. She was a very pretty girl, he realized, but he felt surprise that Will had chosen her. Didn't his brother know she got people into scrapes? She was too lively and willful, and acted without thinking. Look how she'd changed his life, with all she'd done since she carried him off. What would she not do to Will?

He frowned at her, but only for a moment. He must remember that she had a good warm heart and was deeply devoted to anyone she loved. She had proved that by her loyalty to her father and her constant admiration of him. Her happy face had just shown that she thought a lot of Will. She'd be fine for him.

"Aren't you pleased? You—you haven't said a thing." Her eyes were anxious. Was this his cocksure pen companion, Emily Jane? "You look cross, too," she declared, with a most uneasy glance at Mr. Thrace, as if pleading for help from him.

"Oh, but I'm not!" Len smiled to reassure her. He turned to his stepfather. He knew how to talk to him now. He was as close to Len as Will and his mother were, and always had been, only he hadn't seen it. "D'you know what I think, sir? I think she's going to be perfect in our family."

With a delighted cry, Emily Jane seized him for a hug. As she wound her arms around him, the long hair on her tippet pushed into his mouth.

What a girl, he thought. Something unexpected always happens. Now I've got my mouth full of fur!